7.95

· LONDON ·
CONFIDENTIAL
#3

D0249683

THIS ITEM IS DISCARDED BY
REDWATER PUBLIC LIBRARY

dance!

nice shoes!

dress up!

imagine!

Tyndale House Publishers, Inc., Carol Stream, Illinois

Don't Kiss Him Good-bye

Sandra Byrd

beautiful!

Visit Tyndale's exciting Web site at www.tyndale.com.

Visit Sandra Byrd's Web site at www.sandrabyrd.com.

TYNDALE and Tyndale's quill logo are registered trademarks of Tyndale House Publishers, Inc.

Don't Kiss Him Good-bye

Copyright © 2010 by Sandra Byrd. All rights reserved.

Cover photo of girl taken by Stephen Vosloo. Copyright © by Tyndale House Publishers, Inc. All rights reserved.

Cover image of London © by Complete Gallery/Shutterstock. All rights reserved.

Cover image of London seal © by Oxlock/Shutterstock. All rights reserved.

Designed by Jennifer Ghionzoli

Edited by Stephanie Voiland

Published in association with the literary agency of Browne & Miller Literary Associates, LLC, 410 Michigan Avenue, Suite 460, Chicago, IL 60605.

Some Scripture quotations are taken from the Holy Bible, New Living Translation, copyright © 1996, 2004, 2007 by Tyndale House Foundation. Used by permission of Tyndale House Publishers, Inc., Carol Stream, Illinois 60188. All rights reserved.

Some Scripture quotations are taken from the Holy Bible, *New International Version,*® *NIV.*® Copyright © 1973, 1978, 1984 by Biblica, Inc.™ Used by permission of Zondervan. All rights reserved worldwide. www.zondervan.com.

This novel is a work of fiction. Names, characters, places, and incidents either are the product of the author's imagination or are used fictitiously. Any resemblance to actual events, locales, organizations, or persons living or dead is entirely coincidental and beyond the intent of either the author or the publisher.

For manufacturing information regarding this product, please call 1-800-323-9400.

Library of Congress Cataloging-in-Publication Data

Byrd, Sandra.
  Don't kiss him good-bye / Sandra Byrd.
    p. cm. — (London confidential ; #3)
  Summary: Seattle fifteen-year-old Savvy Smith feels like the only girl in England with no date for the traditional May Day Ball, but when she meets a boy with a reputation for trouble, she struggles to follow her own advice.

  ISBN 978-1-4143-2599-6 (sc)

  [1. Schools--Fiction. 2. Advice columns—Fiction. 3. Christian life--Fiction.
4. Balls (Parties)—Fiction. 5. Dating (Social customs)—Fiction. 6. Americans—England--London—Fiction. 7. London (England)—Fiction. 8. England—Fiction.]
I. Title. II. Title: Do not kiss him good-bye.
  PZ7.B9898Dnn 2010
  [Fic]—dc22   2010025039

Printed in the United States of America

16   15   14   13   12   11   10
 7   6   5   4   3   2   1

FOR SAMUEL BYRD,

the son every mother hopes for.
A good boy who grew into a good man.

Chapter 1

It was just a kiss. I saw him give her a simple kiss, a quick kiss, an innocent peck . . . *because they were saying good-bye and no one was watching.*

But someone *was* watching them—me. Not that I'd meant to. I didn't know why the kiss troubled me, but it did. I hid it well, though. Or so I thought.

"Hey, Savvy." Penny waved as she walked toward me, while her boyfriend ducked into his classroom at our school, Wexburg Academy, just outside of London. I'd left Seattle for England less than a year ago, but I was already starting to feel both American *and* British. Some things were very different here—people ate foods like blood sausage and jam butties, and of course there were the school

1

uniforms. Some things were the same here and in the USA, though. We all spoke English, for starters. Classes weren't all that different, and no matter where you were, the high school world pretty much revolved around friends and social groups. And girls in both places had boyfriends. Some did, anyway. Like my new best friend, Penny.

"Hey, Pen," I said. "Good weekend with Oliver?" I nodded toward the door her boyfriend had just walked through.

She blushed, realizing, I supposed, that I had seen *the kiss*. "I went over to his house and helped him with history, and he helped me memorize Spanish phrases." She slung her book bag over her shoulder as we headed down the hall toward our first-period classes. "Oh, and we decided on our colors for the May Day Ball. His mum made the most fabbo biscuits, but I only ate a few. I don't want my dress to be too snug."

"What?" I knew I sounded stupid, but I wasn't sure what she was talking about.

"Biscuits, you know, *cookies*."

"No, no," I said, "I mean, about the May Day Ball. What is it?" We stopped in front of her first-period class, which was a few doors down from my class, maths.

"Oh, that's right—you haven't been here for a May Day Ball yet. Well, it's a big event that's held on May 1, kind of a British tradition to welcome spring and all. It's a really big deal. Everyone dresses up and we rent limousines and have dinner together, and then there are events the day after. It's brilliant—everyone makes sure they have a date months and months in advance because no one wants to miss out. . . ."

She stopped talking then, realizing, I suppose, that *I* was going to miss out, as *I* had no date. Actually, I had never had a date of any kind, although I felt certain that my parents would have given the stamp of approval for me to go to a school-sponsored dance. If someone would have asked me, that is. Months and months ago, of course. The warning bell rang; we had one minute to be in our seats.

"See you at lunch?" she asked.

I shook my head. "I've got to get to the library to print a paper that's due today. I forgot to print it out at home this morning."

"I'll meet you there afterward, then." She threw me her friendliest smile, trying to make up for her faux pas about the May Day Ball.

Chin up, I told myself. *Mustn't grumble. Be British. Or at least British-American.*

I ran to maths and slid into my seat just before the bell rang. I gave a little wave to Hazelle—my sometimes friend, sometimes enemy on the newspaper staff. She ignored me. I looked sideways at Brian, my gum-chewing buddy. He smiled at me, and I smiled back. While Mr. Thompson droned on about domains, reference functions, and formulas, I clandestinely checked out Brian from the corner of my eye.

A few zits—but otherwise a pretty fair complexion. No one I'd jump off a bridge for, but a decent guy, a good conversationalist. He might look awkward in a suit, and I couldn't say for sure if he could dance, but he was a friend who would be fun to spend a few hours with.

At a May Day Ball, of course.

Chapter 2

I headed into the library at lunch. All the computers were taken, so I hung out and waited until I could get one and print out my paper.

One guy seemed like he was ready to wrap things up, so I positioned myself kind of close to his computer. I must have kept glancing over his shoulder to see if he was almost finished because he finally turned and said softly, "What do you think of it?"

I stammered, "Um . . . what do you mean?"

"You've been standing so close for so long, I assumed you must be interested in what I'm writing. Or in me." He flashed a smile—one that disarmed me and drew me in but also felt just the tiniest bit too charming.

"I'm sorry. I just need to print out a paper that's due after lunch."

He saved his document and logged off. Then he stood up and swept his arm with a flourish toward the empty chair. "By all means, you must turn in your paper on time."

I wasn't sure if he was mocking me or appreciating my dilemma, but I took the computer. "Thank you," I said.

"Rhys," he said, "My name's Rhys." His blond hair was pulled back in a neat, short ponytail, but it didn't look weak or feminine at all. Neither did the tiny diamond chip earring he wore in direct defiance of the dress code. His eyes were clear blue. Sled dog blue. Normally I didn't go for blue-eyed blonds. Normally.

Chapter 3

After school I headed over to the Wexburg Academy *Times* office. Officially, I was the school paper delivery girl. Unofficially, undisclosed, I was the author of the school's newly popular advice column. Only Jack, the paper's senior editor, was in on the secret. Oh, and Julia, Hazelle's older sister, who was studying journalism at Oxford. Hazelle both idolized and resented her older sister. If Hazelle ever found out that I, the unstudied American, was the voice behind the Asking for Trouble column, our fragile friendship would be asking for trouble indeed.

"Hullo, Savvy," Jack said. "We'll be running a few extra papers this week since circulation is up. It might take you a bit longer to have them all delivered by half seven on Thursday. You might want to consider starting a bit earlier?"

"Righto." I adopted the old-fashioned British phrase, intending it to be a bit tongue in cheek. Of course, since everyone else in the room was British, no one got the joke.

Jack slid up next to me, close. At one time that would have sent a thrill through me. But now that I knew he was going out with my mentor, Melissa, I made sure the enthusiastic fans in my head stayed in their seats. Truthfully, my crush on him had already been pretty much crushed out.

"We're getting quite a few questions for Asking for Trouble," he whispered in my direction. "I'm having a hard time sorting through them and keeping up with my own work. Is it all right if I simply forward all the questions directly to your e-mail?"

"Of course," I said, keeping my voice and excitement low so as not to draw attention. Inside, I was rejoicing. Each week Jack seemed to recognize my worth more. Soon enough I'd be writing articles with my own name on them—*a byline!* I wouldn't be limited to the secret column anymore. I just knew it.

"I e-mailed the new column to you last night,"

I said. Now that I knew about the May Day Ball and what a big deal it was, I understood the motivation behind the writer's question a little better. In light of my own situation, I was glad I'd given her reassurance.

I hoped.

"I got it," he said. "Good work!" Then he headed back into his own office and closed the door before getting on the phone.

I walked over to Melissa. "You okay?" I asked. Her face looked a little ashy, and her hair was pulled back into a messy ponytail—not her normal, put-together style.

"Feeling a bit dodgy," she admitted. "I woke up not feeling well, and then when I showed up to finish up my article today, I had to help Natalie, too."

"Natalie?" I asked.

"Yes," Melissa said. "She used to live here; worked on the newspaper staff last year. When she moved to the North last summer, it opened up a spot on the newspaper staff."

Ah, yes. The one I took, even though I wasn't officially writing yet.

"She just moved back," Melissa said. She'd never gossip, but I could tell by her tone and the

9

look in her eyes that she would have preferred if Natalie had remained in the North. "She's pushed Jack for an assignment, and I suppose her seniority means she deserves one. She'll be working on the May Day Ball story."

Before that minute it hadn't crossed my mind to ask for the assignment. Now chances were I wouldn't be going . . . or writing about it. I sighed. Loudly, I guess, because Melissa looked up.

"Not going to the ball?" she asked.

I shook my head. "You?"

She nodded.

"Jack?"

She nodded again and smiled, her face brightening for the first time that day. "I'm going to make sure you get to participate in the May Day Ball reporting," she said, a firm look settling like hardening concrete on her face. "If you want it, that is."

I quickly considered my options. I'd get to work on the article, take another step forward on the paper, and have an excuse to go to the ball without feeling like an outcast for not having a date. All positives. I'd also have to work with an unknown, potentially nasty reporter that even Melissa didn't like. One negative.

"Well, Savvy?" Melissa pressed.

"I'll do it," I said.

"Good! And even if you do get a date, you can still gather information beforehand and report and take some snaps on site." But the look on her face betrayed her true beliefs. She didn't think I'd get a date to the ball. It was too late.

That just left me and the unmet Natalie. Both solo.

Chapter 4

The next day I got a text midway through third period. It was from Melissa.

Home sick today. I've sent you an e-mail with my article in it. I need you to hand-deliver it to Jack because I've texted him and he's not answering. Okay?

I texted her back.

Okay, will do.

Brilliant. Back to bed for me, then.

After third period I headed to the library. All the computers were taken again. Right away I saw

Rhys; it would be hard to miss the neat ponytail now that I knew whom it belonged to. I purposely ducked into the library shelves for a few minutes to wait him out and then stood kind of close to another computer, this one occupied by a girl who looked like she was finishing up.

Rhys turned and grinned at me. "Back again, eh?"

I smiled in spite of myself. "Have to print out an article for a friend on the newspaper staff."

"Ah." He nodded. "A journalist. I like journalists. And I just knew you were one of those bright girls. It's not every girl who can be both a brainbox *and* pretty."

It was a totally playerish thing to say. But he called me a *journalist*. And he said it so sweetly, and I basked in the compliment because, you know, they were as few as my officially published word count in the WA *Times*. In other words, nonexistent. I was "bright" enough not to say anything in response, and he turned back to his work. The girl whose computer I'd been waiting for got up, and I took her seat. I checked to make sure no one was looking over my shoulder and logged into my e-mail. I got Melissa's article and sent it to the printer. By the time I logged off and turned around, Rhys was right behind me.

"I don't think I got your name," he said softly.

"Savannah." I didn't know why I gave him my full name instead of saying, "Savvy." I guess I wanted to impress him, to come across as smart as he believed me to be. I caught his eye, and—sorry for the cliché, but it's true—my heart did skip a beat.

"An American, I'd guess, by the accent," he said.

I stood and gathered my gear into the new bag Penny had scored for me at the recent Peter Chen fashion show.

"I'm a foreigner too, sort of," he said.

"You are?" I turned back toward him.

He nodded, and for the first time I noticed that the look on his face was kind of vulnerable. "I'm Welsh," he said. "Moved here last year."

Instantly I felt a kind of bond with him. I let myself relax a little. He must have noticed because he smiled more warmly. "With all the papers you're printing out, it seems like you're pretty good at that kind of work."

I shrugged a little, hoping to seem appropriately modest. "I guess so."

"Would you be willing to look over one of my papers before I turn it in? I know it's a lot to ask, but I don't know a lot of people here yet—certainly no other journalists. I'm trying to catch up on my work. Wexburg Academy is a lot further ahead than my old school was."

I thought for a minute. I mean, what would it cost me, really? a lunch period or something, right? It's not like it was a long-term commitment. And I did like to help people.

"Sure," I said.

"Thank you!" Rhys smiled at me again. "Thursday in the library during lunch?"

I nodded, and as I did, one of his friends came and chipped him on the shoulder. "Let's go, mate," he said impatiently. I noticed that all female eyes locked on Rhys as he left the room. Then they looked at me—I wasn't sure if it was appraisingly or a little jealously. It wasn't a bad feeling to be the envy of the other girls in the room.

I got the paper from the printer and noticed Penny standing at the door of the library. She frowned. "Talking to Rhys, I see?"

"He asked for help with his paper."

She remained silent for a minute while we

headed toward fourth period. "I didn't know you knew him."

"We just met yesterday," I said. "Is something wrong?"

"No, no. He's just . . . not like you, Savvy."

I laughed and gave her a quick hug. "I'm just helping a new kid with his paper. Nothing more."

She relaxed a bit at that. "All right, then."

"Thanks, *Mum*." I teased her to a grin before we parted. "See you sixth period."

Chapter 5

That afternoon I strolled through the showers that promised May flowers, all the while twirling my unopened brolly like a majorette's baton. I was from Seattle. And now I was a Londoner. A little rain wasn't going to melt me. I loved the clean feeling of the drops sliding down my face and into the corner of my mouth, pelting my blonde hair, and slipping off my starched plaid uniform skirt. I turned down Cinnamon Street, past the neat brick houses and window boxes—some newly planted. I left the umbrella propped against our door. A brass plaque announced that I was home: Kew Cottage. I kicked off my shoes, and they went twirling and clattering onto the small porch as I headed inside.

"Pip-pip, cheerio, and all that," I hollered. I heard the back door slam, the one that led out to the small "garden," as the Brits call their patch of patio and backyard. I strolled into the kitchen and saw my sister, Louanne, drying off her arms.

"What were you doing outside?" I asked. Her dog, Giggle (aka Growl), was on the back of the sofa sitting sphinxlike, his paws in front and head up, so I knew she hadn't been taking him out.

Louanne faced me. "Nothing."

She was lying. Hmm, I could coax it out of her so I'd have some blackmail material to make her do my chores. . . . Kidding! But it wasn't like Louanne to flat-out lie to me. I wondered what was up.

"Nothing?" I looked at her face. It was kind of red. A little puffy around the eyes.

She sniffed a couple of times. "Nothing!" she said in a tone that warned me not to ask more questions.

"Okay. Whatever you say." I didn't say anything more even when she went directly to the downstairs loo and washed her hands for a good two minutes. Even Growl lifted his head and looked toward the bathroom before settling down to continue staring out the window at nothing.

20

I grabbed a bowl of Weetabix cereal and a pack of Smarties—the British chocolate kind, not the chalky American kind—from the kitchen and headed into the living room. Growl gave me a dirty look when I plopped down on the couch, but hey—who was the human here? "Sorry, dude. Move over." To be nice, because I'd had a great day, I threw a piece of Weetabix at him. He gobbled it up and returned to his perch.

I opened the *Wexburg Register* and started scanning. Of course, I read the Dear Auntie Agatha column first. Her advice was pretty good that day, if I may say so myself. The old girl still had the go juice in her. Then I turned the page and saw several ads for dresses. Fancy dresses. For the May Day Ball, no doubt. One was for the Marks & Spencer nearby, one for Miss Selfridge in Kensington, which I loved. Another was for a shop in our village. It caught my eye, and I folded the paper back to read it more closely.

Wexburg Register

Looking for a just-right gown for May Day? Have a look at our offerings at the Be@titude Shoppe. We've got the latest designs and only one dress of each style, so you won't look like anyone else at the ball. In addition, a portion of every sale goes to support a local fund-raiser for low-income mums.

My heart tripped like a high heel snagged on an uneven sidewalk. So unfair. I mean, if anyone would appreciate both fashion *and* helping others, it was—

At that moment, Louanne snatched the paper from my hand.

"Hey!" I said. "What are you doing?"

She folded the paper back to the front page and then tossed it in my direction with a snort of disgust. "I thought this was the Wexburg Academy *Times*. Not the local paper."

I caught the paper as it fluttered in my direction. Giggle had had enough, and he jumped off the couch, slinking toward the kitchen. "Since when are you interested in the WA *Times*?"

"Well, uh, since you're interested in it, of course I am too," Louanne said. "I mean, anything you like, I like. Right? You're my big sister and all."

I raised an eyebrow. Louanne didn't know I wrote for the paper, just that I delivered it. "Cool! So when do you want to work on a new look for your wardrobe?"

Louanne wrinkled her nose and shook her head.

"Want to learn to play the guitar?"

She shook her head some again, harder this

time. She was going to get dizzy soon. "Just bring me a paper on Thursday, okay?"

"Okay," I agreed, and with that, she ran upstairs and closed her door.

I headed back to the kitchen and put my cereal bowl in the sink. Growl was sniffing the bags and jackets hanging by the back door. I stared out the window toward the garden. Ours was completely overgrown with ivy and other untended greenery. The smattering of stringy plants looked like Louanne's hair the morning she had woken up with gum tangled in it.

My mom came in and set a couple of bags on the kitchen table. "It's a real mess out there, isn't it?"

I nodded. "Nothing like your garden in Seattle." My mom had been famous for her neatly tended garden.

She sighed. "I know. I bought a few geraniums to freshen up the window boxes in the front, but I don't dare pull any plants back there to do anything else. After all, the yard and house belong to Aunt Maude."

Aunt Maude wasn't really our aunt; she was a friend of our grandmother and was renting this house to us. She wasn't so bad, but she was pretty unpredictable. We never knew what was going to set her off.

"She probably has some dead bodies buried in the back garden. Best not to disturb them and dig up trouble."

Mom came over and gave me a playful swat, and we laughed. "Can you put these groceries away? I want to plant the flower boxes so they're blooming by May."

My mind wandered as I tried to stuff the groceries into our tiny fridge. Ah, May. . . . I imagined it now—I'd find the perfect dress at Be@titude. No one else would have it, of course. I'd arrive just a little late to the May Day Ball on the arm of . . . well, on the arm of someone. Penny would be so glad for me. In fact, we'd probably double-date. Afterward, I'd joke about how I'd worried that I would get to my sixteenth birthday without a first kiss, but clearly . . .

"Savvy!" My mom jiggled my elbow a little. "Are you daydreaming again? You dropped two eggs on the floor!"

"Sorry, Mom." I went to get a rag. Even Growl seemed to roll his eyes at me. Then I headed upstairs to work on my composition paper. I wondered what Rhys's composition paper—the one he wanted my help on—was about.

Chapter 6

The next day I sat with the Aristocats at lunch. It's not like I was a member of the popular crowd—not even on probation, really. But I was good friends with Penny, and Penny had perfect Aristocat lineage. So they tolerated me, anyway. Penny munched on her protein bar. There was an unwritten list of very few "allowable" Aristocat lunch items that you were supposed to commit to memory. Protein bars, energy drinks (diet, of course), cut vegetables, bottles of water. Everything else was frowned upon. I was usually starving by the time I got home. And tonight I wouldn't have time for a quick stop at Fishcoteque for some fish-and-chips first.

"I'm going to the coffeehouse at my church tonight," I told Penny.

"Brilliant—a coffeehouse at church," Penny said. "Not that I've ever been to one. We don't go to church much. Ever, actually."

I knew I should have invited her right then. It was an opening, and I, as a Christian, was supposed to be looking for those things. But it felt weird. I didn't want her to come when I was still as geeky as a newborn calf there. Once I knew a lot of people and felt at home, *then* I'd invite her. "I'll let you know how it goes," I said. "Want to do Fishcoteque after school tomorrow? I won't be at lunch, so I'll be good and hungry."

"Why won't you be at lunch?" she asked.

"I'm meeting with Rhys to help him with his paper."

Penny slowly crumpled the protein bar wrapper, got up to throw it in the dustbin, and silently sat next to me.

"You have a great way of showing your disapproval without saying a word," I noted. "He's a new kid. He needs help. He hangs out in the library during lunch just like I used to because he hardly knows anyone."

"Wherever did you get that idea?" Penny said. "He's been here longer than you, and you manage fine. And he hangs out in the library during his fourth period because he's on academic suspension. I know because he's in my maths class. He has second lunch."

I shrugged it off. One of the things I prided myself on was being a fine judge of character. After all, I'd picked Penny, hadn't I? I, too, could neatly and quietly fold up my protein bar wrapper and then throw it into the rubbish bin without a word. It was the first time I'd been really irritated with Penny. But I felt justified. *Really.*

On the way out of the cafeteria, I walked by the newspaper table, and Melissa stopped me.

"Here, Savvy," she said, handing over a beautiful, leather-bound Wexburg Academy *Times* notebook. It wasn't quite a pen—those were saved for writers with bylines—but it was definitely a sign of acceptance. "Since you'll be an information stringer with Natalie for the May Day Ball, I thought you deserved this to take notes in. Jack agreed."

I looked over at him, and he grinned. He knew I deserved one for the Asking for Trouble column. "Thanks, Melissa." I hugged her, amazed at how she could always find a way to do something kind.

"You can meet Natalie before you deliver

the papers tomorrow morning," she said. Her smile disappeared. Even Hazelle looked away at that.

Chapter 7

My dad was going to drive me to church that night, which was fine, although I probably would have been less nervous if it had been Mom, but she was going to a book club meeting with our next-door neighbor Vivienne. Not that Dad did anything wrong. Moms were more reassuring in situations where you felt unsure of yourself, didn't know anyone, or just needed an emotional pat on the head. But maybe I needed a little push into the pool, and Dad was better for that.

"You coming?" he called to Louanne. Once again, she was mooning around by the back door. It was odd. Had she suddenly acquired Mom's interest in gardening?

"Um, no. I think I'll stay here. Giggle might need me."

Dad and I both looked at her quizzically before I spoke up. "Church is only like twenty to thirty minutes away. Growl probably won't move from the back of the couch."

"Still," she insisted. We locked her in and took off.

"Nervous?" Dad asked.

"Oh, a little," I said. "I know Supriya, though, and I can just hang out in the back and do nothing for a couple of months until I get to know more people. Lie low. You know." I sounded more reassured than I felt. *"Fake it till you make it,"* Grandma Trudy used to say.

Pretty soon we pulled up in front of the church. It had taken us a few church visits and mishaps before we'd found a place we felt comfortable. We'd been going Sunday mornings for a couple of months, but it was a big church, and I felt lost in the crowd. I was hoping to make a few Christian friends, and Supriya had told me it was easier to do that on Wednesday nights. As Madame Antoinette, my French teacher would say, *"Et voilà."* Here I was.

"Go get 'em, Tiger," Dad said.

I smiled weakly. I was not in the mood for geek encouragement.

I walked into the building and headed toward the youth group area. I could smell the coffee— not tea, like they usually had in this country, but coffee. *Thank You, Lord, for a little encouragement.* My former hometown, Seattle, was known for its coffee. I had felt confident and welcome in my church there. The nutty roasted perfume floating through the building reminded me of that and gave me a boost.

I walked into the room and stood there for a minute getting my bearings. Almost immediately, Supriya spied me from across the room and came running over. She didn't have on a sari, which she often wore on Sundays. Her purple sweater over dark blue jeans was perfectly suited to her creamy skin, and tiny diamonds sparkled from her nose and ears. "Come on," she said. "Let's find a good seat before everyone and their cat arrives. The best seats are on the soft couches."

She pulled me over to a corner where a few people were already drinking coffee. One guy clowned around and let the foam from his latte make a white Colonel Sanders mustache. Supriya introduced me to everyone and then ran off to get a refill on her coffee. I held our places; I'd get a mocha when she got back.

"Hi, Savvy, my name's Joe." One of the youth leaders held out his hand, and we chatted for a while. Turned out he was on the praise team—I remembered seeing him up there playing the guitar.

"I play guitar too," I offered.

"Really? What do you like to play?"

"Oh, some worship music. And Taylor Swift. I like her because she writes her own stuff. And because she writes about stuff that I can relate to and understand."

He and I talked music for a few minutes before he said, "Would you ever consider playing guitar on the worship team?"

How could he have known that was a dream I'd had? "I'd love to!" I said. I didn't normally like being in the spotlight, but I figured when you're up there with the whole worship band, it's easy to melt into the whole group.

"Great," he said. "I'll keep it in mind next time we're thinking about adding a guitarist."

After that our conversation drifted off. I felt someone sit down on the couch next to me. I turned to tell Supriya that I would get my coffee from the barista at the cart in the back. But when I looked, it wasn't her. "You're not Supriya!" I realized how idiotic it sounded as soon as it came out of my mouth. But the guy sitting next to me didn't make fun of me.

He smiled and shook his head. "Nope. Sorry to disappoint."

Chapter 8

I almost blurted out that there was no way I was disappointed, but I stopped the words just in time. I replaced them with a cool, "Hi, Tommy. I never noticed you here before."

"You sure do know how to build a lad's confidence." I was pretty sure there was a touch of playful teasing in his grin.

"I'm sorry," I said. "I'm pretty new here."

"And it's a big place," he said. "I understand. Don't like coffee?"

I looked around, and everyone else was holding a mug or a takeaway cup. "I love coffee. I'm originally from Seattle, the birthplace of Starbucks. I was just saving a spot for Supriya until she got back."

"I'll get one for you." He stood up. "What do you like?"

"Mocha?" I said hopefully. "No whipped cream," I added. Drat those Aristocats. Their diet rules had even infected my coffee habits. But it was too late to take it back. Next time, extra whipped cream. Even if it showed up as a slight muffin top later.

"Sure," he said.

As Tommy left, Supriya came back. "You know each other?" She nodded at his retreating back.

"We go to school together," I said as coolly as I could. "And I met him at one of my sister's dog shows." The truth was, every time I'd bumped into him at school, we talked a little longer and I liked him a little better than before.

"You're red in the face, Savvy," she teased. "If I didn't know better, I'd say you fancied him."

I prided myself on avoiding little white lies lately, after my share of missteps in this area. So even though I wanted to deny it, I said nothing.

Tommy came back in a couple of minutes. He looked around quickly out of the corner of his eye. I wasn't sure if he was looking for a place to sit on the overcrowded couches or if he was looking for someone else to talk with. "Here you are," he said, holding out my coffee. He didn't let go of the cup till I took it firmly in my hand. Which meant our hands touched for a brief second.

Savvy, you sap, I thought. *Your hands touched on a coffee cup? Oh, boy. Get a life.* The fans in my heart's inner stadium were doing the wave, though, and I didn't make them sit down.

"Thank you," I said, hoping to reflect a calm I didn't feel. As good of a friend as Supriya was becoming, I wished she'd find something else to do right then—just for a minute—away from this particular couch. She was dead to the vibe, though, and deep in conversation with someone else.

"Still waiting to read something from you in the newspaper." Tommy slowly walked toward a group of his friends and waved good-bye to me.

I took a moment to savor that. *He's been reading the paper looking for my name!* I almost blurted out my secret, that I *was* in the paper every other week, writing the popular Asking for Trouble column. I'd never wanted to tell anyone as much as I did right then.

We stood when the music started—thankfully a worship song I already knew—and soon enough I was deep in the music. I closed my eyes so I could connect better with the Lord. It was a little strange to be worshiping with people in London—people who'd originally come from all over Great Britain, from India, China, Australia, and Africa. And me, from America. I guess before I came to London, I'd always just kind of pictured Christians as Americans.

Goofy, I had to admit now. But my world had been that small. And now it was not.

After a couple more songs, we sat on the couches again while the youth pastor spoke.

"As you know, it's April 1 in a couple of weeks." A big groan went through the crowd. I wondered why. After all, early April brought half-term school breaks, Easter, and lots of holiday time.

"Not this year, please; please, no," someone called out, and a laugh ran through the room.

"Ah, yes, this year will be no exception," Joe said. "Last year we had a lot of smashing entries. And a couple of dodgy ones too. But that makes it fun, right?"

"Rubbish," a guy on the other side of Supriya muttered.

"What's going on?" I whispered to Supriya. She nodded toward the stage.

"In case you're new here in the last year, and I know several of you are, let me explain what the groans are about. Every year the youth group sponsors an 'April Fools for Christ' day the first week of April. Brave souls venture forward to offer a talent—singing, reciting, reading, a skit, whatever—to do in front of the group. In the back of the room we have lidded boxes with a performer's name on each one. Afterward, we add up the money donated in each box. Whoever has the most donations gets to decide which charity all the money will be donated to."

Joe gave a few more details on the event before launching into a short lesson, and then we dissolved into small groups. Supriya's discipleship leader, Jenny, who was at university, invited me to join their group. I wondered if Supriya had mentioned it to her. Either way, I was glad, and I thanked God for Supriya.

"Anyone going to volunteer for April Fools?" Jenny asked after we wrapped up the Bible discussion.

To my surprise—and delight—Supriya volunteered. "I'm going to read a poem in Hindi this year." She mentioned a local children's charity she wanted to sponsor. Jenny gave her a big grin and wrote her name down.

"I am totally going to support you with my

donation," I said. She smiled and we inputted each other's numbers into our phones before getting ready to leave.

I'd nearly made it to the door when Joe grabbed my arm. "Hey, Savvy, I have a great idea. Why don't you do a song on your guitar for April Fools for Christ? The practice sessions would be an amazing way to get to know people. And it'll give the worship team a chance to hear your guitar playing."

He looked so pleased with himself and happy to be helping me out. I felt like saying no, but as I was about to politely decline, I sensed that I should say yes instead. Was it faith? or idiocy? "Okay."

"Brilliant!" Joe whipped out a notebook—which reminded me that I was supposed to be carrying mine around to take notes in—and asked, "What charity would you like to support, then?"

Charity? I had no idea. I didn't even know any charities. Then the ad I'd seen in the paper flashed through my mind. "How about Be@titude?" I offered. "I think they do charities for homeless mothers and stuff."

"Fantastic. The woman who runs it is a Christian, and our church already supports them a little. Good choice. We'll talk more next week about the guidelines for the song selection. See you then!" And with that, he and his notebook were off.

Dad was waiting for me as I exited the church. I laughed aloud as I remembered what I'd told him on the way there. *I can just hang out in the back and do nothing for a couple of months until I get to know more people. Lie low. You know.*

Ha! For better or worse, there would be no lying low now. I was going to be in the wretched spotlight, playing guitar, in three weeks.

Chapter 9

The next morning I got to school early, as I'd promised Jack I would. Starting this week, we had a couple of new spots around campus to put the newspaper. I was especially glad to have a great delivery bag today because I knew I'd be meeting . . . Natalie.

I walked into the newsroom, and she and Melissa were already there. Natalie was sitting at the one computer station that had been open since I'd joined the staff. I had been hoping that station would eventually be mine. I'd already planned it out—I would take all the junk off the desk and tidy everything up. I'd cover the tired wallpaper behind the station with some amazing fashion clips, a few motivational quotes from

43

the Society of Professional Journalists, my beach-themed Son Worshiper button, and perhaps my melded American-British flag poster from home. In no time at all, it'd be the place everyone gathered to plot out and plan the next issue of the paper.

"Savvy!" Melissa's voice snapped me out of my reverie. "Are you okay?"

I shook myself out of my daydream and answered in as focused a voice as I could muster. "Oh yeah, I'm fine."

"I was just telling Natalie that you'll be working with her on the May Day Ball story."

"She'll be gathering information for *my* story, right?" Natalie said.

"Savvy has a lot of good ideas," Melissa said. "I think she'd have a lot to offer." But she didn't force anything on her, and I knew this wasn't going to be easy. I was going to have to earn my spot. Besides, I had the Asking for Trouble column. Even if I wrote it secretly at home. Alone.

"Hey." I offered my hand for Natalie to shake it, but she ignored it.

"I've written up some guidelines—the focus of the article, some of the background information I'll need . . . oh, and we'll need the angle. So you're not going to the ball?" she asked, business straight off.

"No . . . not yet," I said.

She snorted, reflecting the general opinion that if you didn't have a date months in advance, it was not likely to happen. "Fine, then. You can gather some of the background information. And take photos at the event. Melissa led me to believe that you have some useful experience in photojournalism?"

I nodded. *Sigh*. Snapping pics again. But at least I was a stringer doing some interviewing and fact-gathering this time.

"I'll e-mail your assignment to you along with my direction." Natalie glanced at Melissa, who was watching her closely. "And you can send me any ideas you have," she said. With that, she turned to her desk—my fantasy desk—and got back to work. I, on the other hand, loaded the papers into my bag with a little help from Rob, the paper's printer, and Rodney, a year-eleven sports reporter.

I delivered the papers pretty quickly. The day was dry for the middle of March, and the sun warmed the top of my head and spread clear through me. I loved the Thursdays when my column was in the paper. If I had time, I sat down and read it on a bench after delivering them and before first period, savoring the sight of my words in print. It felt good to help others, to let the Lord use me to do the good works He'd prepared in advance for me to do. Even with the additional papers, I had time to plop down on a bench outside the front office and open the last paper in my bag.

Dear Asking for Trouble,
I never thought I'd be writing to an advice column like this. Well, a guy I know has asked me to go out with him next weekend to a huge party in the country. He's cute and nice, and a lot of other girls are jealous. Great, right? Not so much. I know he likes me, but I only consider him a friend. If I accept, I'm afraid he'll think I like him, even though I've told him we're just friends. If I don't go to the party, I'm home alone—again—for the weekend. I've told everyone I don't care about being by myself, that I study a lot. But I do care. What should I do?
Sincerely,
Wishing for More

46

Dear More,
I know it's dull to be home when your friends all seem to be out. But I'm betting there are other girls who are home during the weekends too. Can you ask around and plan a movie night for that weekend? Even though you've tried to tell him you're just friends, he seems to believe otherwise. Guys can be thick! If you go to the party, you might be giving this guy the wrong idea, and you've said he's a friend, right? You don't want to do that if you can help it. Hang in there. The right one will come along. In the meantime—Blu-ray, anyone?

Patiently yours,
Asking for Trouble

I left the paper open and let the sun come down on my face while I thought about that. I sounded so smart and on top of things when I wrote in the column. I wished I were going with someone special too. But I envied her. She had someone to go to the May Day Ball with, if she wanted to, even if he was only a friend. If I had an unattached guy friend, I'd be going too, instead of snapping pics for Natalie.

"New edition?"

I opened my eyes to see Tommy standing over me. The paper was still folded to the Asking for Trouble column.

"Oh . . . yeah," I said, folding the paper and standing up straight.

"You write anything in there?" he asked.

Now what? No one else had ever asked me straight out. And yet I'd promised myself—and Jack—months ago that I wasn't going to tell anyone I was writing the paper's advice column.

"No byline yet," I answered.

"What were you reading?" he asked.

"Asking for Trouble," I said honestly.

"Cool." He slung his backpack over his arm and we headed inside. "Nice to see you at church last night. Are you going to do something for April Fools?"

I nodded. "Joe convinced me to play guitar. You?"

He shook his head. "I'm usually at football practice during the week, so I can't commit to Wednesday nights too often. Also, my mum broke her foot and can't drive for another month or so.

My dad doesn't usually get home from work in enough time for me to make it in the middle of the week." He looked at his watch and then at me. Yes, his eyes were definitely Johnny Depp in *Pirates*. "Talk to you soon." He grinned at me and I melted back—I mean, smiled back—as he ducked into his classroom.

The bell rang. Uh-oh. I was still two hallways away from my class.

Chapter 10

"You're late, Miss Smith." My maths teacher, Mr. Thompson, picked at the mole on his face till it bled and looked disapprovingly at my disheveled appearance. I had just booked it down the hallway. "Detention at lunch or after school today."

I'd promised to meet Rhys to help him with his paper during my lunch hour. I needed to honor my commitment. "After school," I answered.

"Very well." He called the class to attention.

Chapter 11

At lunchtime I made my excuses to Penny, and even to Hazelle, who for some unknown and therefore questionable reason was being very sweet and asked me to sit next to her at lunch. Then I headed to the library to meet with Rhys. When I got there, all the computers were occupied. But not by Rhys. Five minutes later, a computer opened up, and rather than hanging around looking like an idiot, I sat down and logged on to my e-mail. There was a short list from Natalie, as promised, of the things she wanted me to do.

1. Suggest several couples to feature in the paper.

2. Talk to local businesses to see if they'd be interested in sponsoring adverts before the dance.
3. Research the history of May Day.
4. Think through some good picture angles.

I sighed. Research, but no writing. I'd suggest a few story ideas to her. I was hoping that I might be able to do a write-up on Be@titude for the paper, maybe drive some business their way. It was funny—I had never even been there, but just from one simple piece in the newspaper, I was already involved with them on two levels. It was the power of the written word. Which was what I loved about writing.

I looked at the large face clock on the wall. Lunch hour was half over. I logged off and got up from the computer. I wandered the library to see if Rhys was in one of the rows and I had missed him somehow. He wasn't anywhere to be found. A few minutes later I hid in the corner and gobbled my protein bar, then washed it down with water from the drinking fountain. Three minutes before lunch was up, I finally conceded that he'd stood me up. Part of me was mad—I'd wasted a whole lunch, and besides, it never felt good to be left hanging. Part of me was relieved, though. I couldn't pinpoint exactly why, but I was.

On the way to fourth period, composition and literature with Mrs. Beasley, I thought I saw a familiar ponytail duck into the lunchroom. He was laughing with his "mate," the same one I'd seen him with the other day. A gaggle of girls was following them. Rhys sat down at a table facing me, and he spotted me as I was passing through the hallway outside the lunchroom. I kept walking, not wanting to be late for another class.

"Hey, there's my girl Savannah," he called out.

My girl?

Rather than make a scene, I went into the lunchroom and walked over to his table. "Hey—weren't we supposed to meet at the library last period?" *My lunch period,* I wanted to add.

"I am so sorry." Turning to his friends, he said, "Savannah is really smart—and generous, too. She promised to help me with my paper, and I totally forgot. Forgive me?" he asked, turning back toward me. He looked genuine.

Well, I was supposed to forgive, right? "All right," I said, unable to resist as he turned on his charm.

"Tomorrow?" he asked. "I'll type it into my phone right now so I won't forget. I really need your help. And while I'm at it, what's your number?"

I watched as he punched my number into his phone.

"You're the best." He reached over and hugged me just a second longer than absolutely necessary. It felt good to be needed. "See you tomorrow."

As I turned to leave, I glanced at the tables right behind Rhys. It looked like another set of Aristocats. Well, of course, they'd have a set of tables in second lunch too.

A moment later I felt rather than saw someone looking at me. I looked up, and for a second I locked eyes with Tommy. He looked at Rhys, and I wondered if he'd heard the entire exchange. Probably. And no doubt he'd caught the shout-out to "my girl" too. I gave him a feeble little smile, and he smiled back, reserved but friendly. And then he turned back to the girl at his right arm—Chloe; I recognized her from my visit to The Beeches.

She leaned toward him till they were thisclose.

Chapter 12

"You're late, Miss Smith." My composition and literature teacher, Mrs. Beasley, took off her glasses and rubbed them clean as I took my seat in front of the entire class. I was still sucking wind after having run down the hallway.

"Detention after school today," she said, frowning.

"I can't come after school today." The whole class eyeballed me.

"Why not?"

I sighed and told the truth. "I have detention with Mr. Thompson today."

She gave me the *I'm extremely disappointed* look, one I hadn't been used to getting from teachers . . . until lately. She rubbed her tongue over her teeth, sighed, and finally said, "Very well. Tomorrow, then."

Chapter 13

Usually there was nothing like time with my family and at church to refresh my priorities. But the weekend had felt a little off for some reason. Both Louanne and Dad seemed to be coming down with something. Mom thought it was probably allergies because there were new plants blooming in England that neither of them had been exposed to before. Louanne seemed worse off than Dad, which was odd, because except for rabbits, cats, and horses, Dad typically had way more allergies than Louanne.

Sunday the pastor preached through "One and Two" Corinthians. I thought that was cute. At home we'd have called it "First and Second" Corinthians.

"Not riding horses in secret, are you?" I teased Louanne after she sniffled her way through church. "*National Velvet,* maybe?" Ever since we'd moved to London, she'd idolized that movie. But as soon as I said it, Louanne got angry and left the room. *Touchy, touchy.* I wondered if she was just having a rough week or if something else was going on. She wasn't usually so moody. When I was ten, there'd been a mean girl who'd picked on me for a couple of weeks. Was Louanne being bullied at school?

On the way home, I turned on my phone and saw ten texts from Rhys asking where I was. I started texting him back when Louanne elbowed me.

"What?" I was irritated—I'd made two typos. I hated making typos.

"Dad just asked you a question."

I kept reading Rhys's text, and before I could respond, a new one was incoming.

"What do you want?" I asked. The car grew quiet. I felt the silence like ice in my bones.

"Were you talking to *me*?" Dad asked. "Turn off the phone."

Great. I had a feeling I was going to pay for this later, with Rhys.

"Sorry," I said, not really feeling sorry. After all, Dad had interrupted my conversation.

"Who were you texting?" Mom asked.

"Rhys," I said. I saw a look go between her and my dad. But neither said a word.

Chapter 14

As I headed out the door on Monday morning, I noticed Mom's geraniums were starting to pop to life in the flower boxes. The streets were slick with the remembrance of last night's rain, and the world smelled cool and fresh and new. And I have to admit, I had another reason for hope. Last night I'd thought of a wonderful plan.

Before first period I stopped in the newspaper office. Natalie was hard at work at "her" desk, and Melissa and Jack were at theirs.

I stood behind Natalie and asked, "Did you get my e-mail about the May Day stuff?"

Natalie kept typing; she didn't even pause when she responded. "I'm thinking about it, Savvy. I'm just not sure how I want my article to shape up yet. I'll let you know. Send the history of May Day when you can, okay? As for Be@titude, I'm not interested in that religious stuff."

I rolled my eyes. Helping low-income mothers was religious stuff?

I headed to first period, restored to Mr. Thompson's good graces because I'd scored 100 percent on a quiz the day after my detention. He'd been good enough not to suggest that the extra studying at detention had been what pushed me over. We got to work in groups that morning, and I headed over to Hazelle.

"How's the romance coming?" I asked.

She blushed deeply. I was shocked. I'd never seen her blush. She was a no-nonsense reporter. Her face was nearly the color of her lipstick, which I knew to be Ruby Desire. "Oh, I'd hardly call it a romance," she said. "But I suppose the May Day Ball has inspired that kind of thought in nearly everyone."

Just then Brian came up and joined our group. He sat thisclose to Hazelle and . . . I got it! I'd been asking Hazelle about the romance novel she was writing, and *she* thought I meant her relation-ship with Brian. Aha, now I understood why she was in maths early and not at the paper office.

My Brian. Well, not really *my* Brian. But we were gum-chewing, cover-for-you-if-you-cover-for-me friends. And if we'd both understood that we were only friends, it might have been fun to go to the May Day Ball together.

After class I walked toward second period with Hazelle. "I had no idea you and Brian were, um, dating," I said.

She grinned. "We're not . . . not yet, anyway. But he asked me to the ball some time ago, and I said yes. Just as friends. I mean, we both knew we were just friends. But since then we've been talking and texting a lot more, and I'm not sure. He's a really nice guy."

Her voice was so sweet and sincere and happy and . . . soft—for the first time ever. I tried hard not to resent her or be jealous. "I'm very glad for you," I said.

"Do you have a date?" she asked hesitantly.

I shook my head. "I'll be helping Natalie with her article about the ball, taking snaps, you know." I tried to force sunshine and butterflies into my voice.

"That's nice," she said. But my journalistic instincts were honed as sharp as acrylic finger-nails. I knew she didn't mean it. But she was trying, and her voice had no edge to it for once, so I let it go.

At lunch Penny tried her best to cheer me up with some new clothes ideas she'd been sketching, and we also planned to get together at her house the next week. Inevitably, though, the conversation at the table turned to the May Day Ball. Apparently all the Aristocats were going shopping for dresses together that weekend.

Penny reached over and gave me a one-armed hug. "I wish you were coming too."

"Bosh, they probably wouldn't want me to come," I said under my breath.

"It'd be okay, really. I think they like you more than they let on."

I zoned out of their conversation and pretended to jot down some important things in my journalism notebook. Actually, I was writing down all the names of boys I'd been at least somewhat interested in, crossing out the ones who turned out to like someone else.

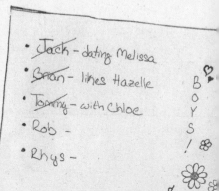

- ~~Jack~~ – dating Melissa
- ~~Brian~~ – likes Hazelle
- ~~Tommy~~ – with Chloe
- Rob –
- Rhys –

B
O
Y
S
!

dance!

Well, there still was Rob. And Rhys. I'd see Rob at the newspaper office. And I'd be finishing Rhys's paper with him at Fishcoteque after school tomorrow.

After lunch was fourth period. I hadn't earned my way into Mrs. Beasley's good graces since last week's detention yet. I think I'd been kind of one of her favorites, and now she was disappointed in me for getting two detentions. Fair enough. I was disappointed in myself.

Chapter 15

"So what'll it be then, luv? The usual?" Jeannie, the server at the local fish-and-chips place, grinned at me from behind the counter. I loved her, and her fish-and-chips, and she knew it and loved me right back.

"The usual," I said. The thought crossed my mind that Rhys might make fun of me for eating a full meal after school, and then I wondered why I even cared if he made fun of me or not. I took my laptop and sat down at my booth, waiting for both of them—Rhys and my order—to arrive.

I worked a little on a paper and did some fact-checking for Natalie; then I pulled up my e-mail. As I typed in my password, I heard Rhys come up behind me. I quickly closed my e-mail.

69

"I'm not late today—did you notice?" he asked as he slid into the opposite side of the booth.

"I noticed," I said with a smile.

Jeannie brought over my fish-and-chips and asked Rhys if he'd like some.

"No thanks," he said. Jeannie sniffed and muttered something about paying her rent with people who lingered but didn't eat. She seemed to have cooled just a tiny bit toward me, and I wondered if it had anything to do with Rhys. He pulled out his paper and handed it to me.

I was impressed. "You've made a lot of good changes." I gave him a few more pointers and then handed the paper back.

"You're a good teacher." He sounded genuine. "I worked on it on Sunday, probably while you smart kids were off having fun."

I splashed one of my chips with malt vinegar. "I was at church on Sunday," I said.

"Ahhh . . . well, then. An American *and* a Christian. By all rights I should hate you. But I don't."

I'd heard of a backhanded compliment before but didn't exactly understand what that meant. Now I did. Did he mean to praise or insult me? I decided to think the best. "Thank you," I said.

70

"You might just change my mind about both," he said. Two girls came into the shop then and waved flirtatiously at Rhys. He lifted a hand politely but didn't flirt back. Instead he turned to me.

I took a bite of fish and considered his last comment. "My church is having a kind of . . . talent show," I said. Something told me not to mention the real name of it: April Fools for Christ. I had the nagging feeling it would provoke a comment that I wouldn't like.

"Oh."

"Maybe you could come," I said. *And hear the gospel*, I thought. I had to admit the tiniest part of me was also hoping he'd come and publicly support me with all those nice things he said about my being smart and pretty and helpful. It would boost my confidence. I wasn't sure why he had the power to swing my feelings so much, both up and down.

"Maybe, Savannah. Maybe. I might just do that." We chatted for a while, and then he spied some of his mates heading to the back of the restaurant, where the dartboard was. "I'd best join the lads," he said. "I promised."

"I've got to get home too," I said. As I closed

up my computer, he leaned close to me. Very close.

"See you soon, Savannah." I could feel him drawing me in somehow. Like a magnet. Then he smiled, his teeth perfectly white and even, and his clear blue eyes looking unblinkingly at me. This time they didn't really seem sled doggish. More like a tiny bit wolfish. But maybe a pet wolf.

On the way home I had a weird song stuck in my head. It was one of Dad's favorites, one we teased him about whenever he put on his golden oldies rotation on his iPod.

Chapter 16

The next night I got to church early to discuss plans for the April Fools for Christ night. I took my guitar, my leather WA *Times* notebook, and my Bible.

"I'm so glad you're here," I said to Supriya. "It'll be really fun to do this together."

Joe wrote up a roster of performers. Even though I'd been planning to say no, I was actually really happy I'd agreed to do this. It was my church. I wanted to get to know people. And I cared about giving to others.

About half an hour later, everyone else started filtering in. I got myself a mocha and wandered around meeting people with Supriya. I also looked around a little. Kind of casually, you know.

Chill. As the worship team went up to the front, Supriya leaned over and whispered, "He's not normally here on Wednesdays."

Startled, I answered, "Who?"

"Tommy."

"Who said I was looking for Tommy?"

She just smiled, the music started, and we began to sing. I closed my eyes.

Was I that obvious? Anyway, Savvy, put it all behind you. He likes Chloe. Focus.

I went home that night and put away all my romance novels. I left the textbooks out where I could see them. And the latest edition of the WA *Times*.

In the middle of the night, I got up again and took one of the romance books back out of the box. It was a Christian romance. A girl had to have hope.

Chapter 17

The next morning I arrived at the Wexburg Academy *Times* office a little early again. I was glad today was a uniform day because only my black uniform shoes got wet. I'd just bought some new UGGs, creamy beige suede on the outside and soft wool on the inside. I was excited to wear them on casual Friday, and I really hoped it wouldn't rain tomorrow.

I walked into the newsroom and breathed in the dusty smell of the newsprint and the acrid smell of the ink, felt the heat of the presses and the glare of the fluorescent lights. My future was calling! And I would answer!

Rob came out from behind his printer. "Need any help loading the papers?" he asked.

"Yeah, thanks—in just a minute." First I had to talk with Jack. I found him standing next to a board with the current issue laid out and pinned up. I leaned in and whispered, "I think there's been some kind of e-mail error. I haven't been getting the forwards."

"Forwards?" he asked in a rather loud voice. He looked distracted. I spotted the reason right away. The current issue had a few typos. He frowned, took out a highlighter, and marked them. I was glad my name was not on any of those bylines.

"For the Asking for Trouble column," I said, trying to keep my voice down. "If I'm going to have time to choose the questions and then write up my answers, I'll need to have them soon. You want the copy by next Tuesday, right?"

"Ah, yes, right," Jack said. "Sorry about that. I'll check on it later this morning."

I turned around, and as I did, I saw Rob standing very close behind me. He met my eyes. They betrayed nothing, but I wondered if he'd been there awhile and heard our conversation.

"Ready?" he asked.

"Yep." Together we stuffed my green-swirled designer bag with papers. "Going to the May Day Ball?" he asked.

I looked up, hopeful. He wasn't really my idea of Prince Charming, but he was a nice guy, and he'd been a good friend to me since I'd joined the newspaper staff. Truth be told, I suspected he was the person who had delivered my anonymous box of chocolates at Valentine's Day. After all, he often did have chocolate in his printing office. And he'd been awfully sweet to me.

"No, I'm not . . . yet," I said. "You?"

He nodded. "I have a girlfriend at another school. She's coming here for the dance. I'll go to her school's Autumn Leaves Ball."

I kept a bright smile on my face—I really did. *Happy thoughts.* "That's great," I said. "Natalie has assigned me to choose some couples to feature in the paper. Maybe I could get your picture?"

"Thanks, Savvy." Rob grinned. "Dahlia would love that. It might make her even appreciate the newspaper life a bit more." He gave me a quick, friendly hug and helped me finish loading the papers.

I dutifully delivered the papers. That's right, that's me. Always the fairy godmother, never Cinderella.

In first period, Brian's and Hazelle's moony eyes were annoying me, so I pulled out my list instead. Only one name was left.

Chapter 18

Louanne attacked me as soon as I got in the front door. "Isn't today the day your paper comes out? Did you bring a copy home for me?" She tugged one of the straps of my green bag, trying to part the folds and peer inside.

"Hold on, cowgirl," I said. "I've got one in here someplace. But let me catch my breath." Even Growl was eyeing her with curiosity. "So what's the big deal with the paper?"

"I told you," she said not very convincingly. "We're sisters. I'm interested in your stuff, just like you're interested in my stuff, like dog shows."

I wasn't sure how she came by that misunderstanding about my liking dog shows, but I let her hang on to it. I threw my messenger bag in the corner, careful not to hit my new UGGs, waiting patiently for their debut the next morning. "So when can I paint your nails?" I asked.

She took both hands and put them around her throat, pretending to choke herself. "Never. But it *was* nice of you to offer to come to the dog show with me this weekend. Thanks, Savvy."

"Anything for you, kid." I handed her the WA *Times*.

She took the paper and ran upstairs, Growl galloping after her, his low-slung belly shaving the carpet.

"You're going to have to lay off the treats if you're going to do dog shows," I called after him. As if he cared.

I headed into the kitchen and pulled out the box of Weetabix. I hadn't even put milk in the bowl yet when Louanne slunk back downstairs. "What's with you? You look like someone pushed you off the bus four stops early."

"Nothing," she said.

"Want to play a game?" I hated to see her so down. Usually a rousing game of Monopoly or Scrabble would cheer her up.

"No thanks," she said.

"Want to talk about animals?" I asked. "You

know, a lot of my friends have two pets—Penny, Hazelle, and Ashley each have two dogs. Maybe you should ask Mom and Dad for a friend for Giggle."

At that, she practically stumbled over the sofa in an effort to get away from me. "Gotta go do my homework. Bye." She bolted from the room again, Giggle wheezing after her.

I headed upstairs and plopped my homework on my dresser. I stared at *Voilà! C'est la France!* and decided I'd better catch up on my French homework later that night. I looked at the pile in the corner—a tossed salad of clothes that I didn't like anymore, that were not very flattering, that were the wrong color, that I didn't want to fold and hoped my mother would rewash and fold for me. Then I looked at my guitar.

Only thirteen days till the April Fools show, I thought. I wondered if Rhys would ask about it again. He might be a little interested in Christianity. Maybe. And this could be the event that helped him see that Christians were normal and fun. I'd better pick my song soon and e-mail it to Joe for his approval.

For some reason, though, I just couldn't get up the desire to play the guitar right then. I watched

BBC on the telly, and then it was dinnertime. Here's how the conversation went:

Dad: "This tomato soup is very good, dear— especially on a rainy night. Are you starting to think about planting your garden?"

Mom: "I'd love to get my hands on the patch out back—I just don't know, though. The property is Aunt Maude's, not mine, and we'd have to dig out so many weeds."

Me: "We can help you weed it, Mom. I'm sure Aunt Maude would be glad to have it all cleared out and prettied up."

Louanne: "I feel sick! Please excuse me!" And she ran from the table, leaving her napkin to flutter to the floor.

Dad looked at Mom and then at me. "What was that all about?"

"I don't know," Mom said. "She's been acting strange lately. I've asked her if everything is okay at school, and she says yes. But she seems to be teary a lot. Savvy, do you know what's up?"

I chewed and swallowed the last rubbery nub of tangy English Cheshire cheese from the bottom of my soup bowl before answering. "Nope. I noticed it too. I'll see if I can find out."

Chapter 19

Late that night, after Louanne was snoozing, Growl curled in a nest of blankets at the foot of her bed. The tinny sounds of late-night telly came from behind my parents' bedroom door, and I sat cross-legged on the floor of my own room. My shiny rosewood guitar—the one big item I was allowed to bring to London from Seattle—sat next to me, quietly, comfortably, like the old, faithful friend it was. I looked through my sheet music. Usually a particular song would call to me from the dotted black staccato of notes bursting on a page. I could hear the music in my head as I read it, begging to be let out. But not now.

I stood and looked out my window. It still got cold at night, and condensation beaded up in the corners of my old-fashioned glass panes. When enough droplets gathered together, they joined strength and coursed down the glass like a tear-drop. I watched them for a minute, then looked out on the neighborhood below.

Lord, I want to play a song that will honor You. One that I really like and can play with feeling. Please help me pick a good one.

My thoughts went from the April Fools show to the May Day Ball, which honestly was never far from my mind.

It's okay if I don't go, I said to myself.

But I really want to, and that's okay too, I said back.

But who could I go with? I replied.

I felt like such a hypocrite for giving such a breezy, know-it-all answer to the girl who'd written in the paper. I watched as the lights shut off in each of the neighborhood houses till only one house was still lit. *Only one choice left, as far as I can see.*

I sat on the floor and searched through the Taylor Swift music again. There was no escaping the fact that certain titles caught my eye more than others. "Love Story." "Baby, Don't Break My Heart." "Sparks Fly."

One song called to me, and as I picked up the music, I knew two things for sure:

1. The Lord had answered my prayer and showed me the song to play. *Thank You, Lord.*

2. The song had a *double entendre,* one of the words in my French homework that night. It meant "a word or expression used in a given context so that it can be understood in two ways."

YOU BELONG WITH ME
by Taylor Swift

Chapter 20

Friday, glorious Friday, when I could wear whatever I wanted to school, when an entire weekend stretched ahead, with sleeping in on Saturday, followed by waffles and scrambled eggs whipped up by my dad. I had homework, of course. And I needed to practice my song for April Fools. Plus, I'd promised Natalie I'd do a bit more research for her. But it was still Friday!

"Love the boots, Savvy," Ashley said as I sat down at the lunch table. The entire table went quiet. Had Ashley just complimented me? I felt her crown of approval on my head. Others must have noticed because I felt a distinct thaw in the attitude toward me at the table. Penny beamed like a proud mum. I felt pretty glad too. I had been myself, had remained true to myself, and that was good enough to be noticed.

"Thank you, Ashley. I love your new bag. Yellow patent leather is very in." I returned her compliment in kind. It was true—she did have a great bag. Then Penny and I got down to business: nibbling the protein bars she'd brought and the bag of veggies I'd brought. I looked at the clock.

Four more hours till I can get to the chippie for my real meal!

"Hey, what are you doing after school?" I asked Penny. "Want to shop in the village with me? I was thinking of checking out Be@titude and then heading to Fishcoteque."

"Brilliant, Savvy, but tonight's the night a bunch of us—" she nodded in the direction of the other Aristocats—"are taking the bus and the Tube to London to shop for dresses. I'm sorry."

"Is Chloe going with you?" I asked, trying to seem as if I didn't really care. Casual. Chill. You know.

"Yes . . . why?"

I shook my head. "No reason; just wondering."

I could see her little-white-lie detector go off, but she was loyal enough not to ask me anything in front of the rest of the group. Instead, she squeezed my hand and then wrote *Monday!* on my hand in Sharpie. "We're still getting together at my house on Monday, right? And my mum would like you to stay for supper."

"Okay. Have a good time," I said, meaning it. I hadn't told her this, but I was definitely, absolutely going to feature her and Oliver as one of the couples in the paper.

After school I dropped off most of my gear at home and headed to the village square with only my purse and my WA *Times* notebook. The daffodils labored to push their heads through the ground, and some of them had successfully burst through in a ground-level shot of sunshine.

I arrived at a tidy brick shop with wide, clean windows and the word *Be@titude* scrawled across the top. The clothes in the window ranged from chic and fresh to fairly modern—nothing stodgy here. I opened the shop door, and the chimes twinkled merrily as I stepped in.

"Hullo, there. How can I help you, then?" a stylish young woman asked.

"My name is Savannah Smith," I said, holding out my hand in the most professional, grown-up manner I could. "I'm a reporter for the Wexburg Academy *Times*. I saw your ad in last week's paper, and I was hoping to do a little write-up on your store for the May Day Ball."

"Ah, that." She looked a bit sad. "Haven't had much business for the ball, I'm sorry to say. I suspect most girls are keen to take the Tube into London and shop at Miss Selfridge, Topshop, and Harrods. Can't say as I blame them. I know it's not as glamorous to shop in town."

She draped a tape measure around her neck, a centimetered boa, and set a box of pumps on the glass counter. "I'm Becky, by the way, the store owner. Come on back and I'll show you the room we use for the ministry."

I was right! This *was* a Christian charity. She used the word *ministry*.

"Back here are the clothes we buy with a percentage of the profits; these go to single mums. Normally they have a hard time making ends meet, right? So it's difficult for them to find enough money to set aside for business clothes and such. But they need them to successfully interview for jobs."

I scribbled furiously, trying to get everything down.

"My idea was to take a bit of the money we make from women and girls who *do* have money for fun clothes, ball gowns, extra fashionable wardrobes, and such, and supply these struggling women with good work clothes."

"How many people have you been able to help?" I asked.

"So far, ten," she said. I could hear the pride in her voice. "We could help dozens more if we had the funds." The front door chimed, and she excused herself to go up front. I looked at the prim but stylish business skirts, slimly elegant and encased in dry cleaner's plastic. Becky had partnered each one with a little bag of accessories.

It would be extremely cool if I could help somehow, I mentioned to the Lord in my head.

"I was hungry, and you fed me. I was thirsty, and you gave me a drink. I was a stranger, and you invited me into your home. I was naked, and you gave me clothing." The response was so clear I turned around to see if some guy had snuck in and actually spoken aloud to me. But I was alone still, in the back room.

"Well, then," Becky said as she returned. "Let me show you the rest of the store and talk about the event we're holding in the beginning of July." As we wandered through the forest of mannequins and wheels of clothing, she shared her heart about building up as many funds as possible and then having a kickoff near Emmeline Pankhurst Day.

"I'd like to help however I can," I offered after jotting down *Emmeline Pankhurst??* in my notebook. "I'm hoping that by putting this in the paper, I can drum up some support for this ministry. . . ." My voice trailed off as I came upon the most wonderful ball gown I'd ever seen. *"Ohhhh . . ."*

Becky laughed. "I can see why you'd like that one. It's called Faeries—it's a new design by a young woman starting out in Kent. The tea green would look just right with your light coloring."

I reached out and gently touched the fabric. Becky held the dress up to me, and we walked together to the three-way mirror. It had a close-fitted halter top with thick straps—modest but lovely. The fabric shimmered under a lace overlay of the same color and finally cascaded into a close, conservative waterfall of froth that halted midcalf.

"With tiny peridot green earrings," I said to no one in particular. "And an updo."

"You're a fashionista besides a journalist," Becky said. She laughed and I reluctantly allowed her to hang the dress back up. "You've got style, anyway. Bought your dress yet?" she asked hopefully.

I shook my head and tried to keep my voice peppy. "Not going—well, just going on assignment, that is." I tapped my journalist's notebook.

"Ah," she said. We locked eyes for a moment and felt the bond of sisterhood between two Christians who had hopes and dreams that seemed to have stalled right over the Bermuda Triangle. Another customer came into her shop, and rather than distract her from people with actual cash to spend, I snapped my notebook shut and headed out.

"I'll let you know when the article appears," I said.

"Thank you, Miss Smith."

"Savvy!" I said, feeling like my own upbeat self again for the first time in a long while.

"Savvy, then." She laughed. "I'm sure we'll get on well." She turned her attention to the two girls who had come into the store looking for ball dresses. I hoped they hated green.

Chapter 21

Night began to fall, and I headed toward Fish-coteque. I texted my mother that I'd be late. She and Louanne had plans for the evening, and my dad was working late, so she didn't mind that I was going to hang out at the chippie to get some writing done. I had all the Asking for Trouble letters to sort through too, and I needed to choose one for next week's column.

I pulled open the door and breathed in the familiar steamy, greasy, fishy smell that signaled my London home away from home.

"Hullo, luv. The usual, then?" Jeannie leaned over the counter and gave my cheek a friendly tweak.

"Yes, please." I withdrew the proper amount

from my British flag coin purse and handed it across the counter. She gave me an ice-cold bottle of orange Fanta and a glass of ice.

"Your young man is here," she whispered.

"Who?"

She pointed to a booth across the room, and I saw who she was pointing to. Rhys.

"He's not my young man. He's just a friend."

"Just as you says." Jeannie nodded.

I started toward another booth, but Rhys waved me over. I'd really wanted some time by myself, but he grinned and managed to look goofy and friendly and cute all at the same time. I headed in his direction even as Proverbs 31:30 ran through my mind; it'd been a memory verse some years back. *Charm is deceptive, and beauty does not last. . . ."*

On my way, I passed a booth with my science buddies Gwennie and Jill in it. "Want to join us?" they asked. I could see they had fashion magazines spread out in front of them.

"Maybe later?" I asked, eager to get to Rhys . . . and possibly my own date for the ball.

"Hey, Savvy, I had no idea you'd be here," he said. But it didn't sound true. After all, I'd been coming to Fishcoteque for months and had never seen him here before the past week or so. "I'm so glad you introduced me to this place." It was like he was somehow able to read my mind and disarm my concerns.

Jeannie delivered my fish-and-chips and mushy peas a few minutes later. I noticed that Rhys was eating this time. "She said no pay, no play. Truth be told, the fish is rather good!" He wiped his hands on a napkin. "No big date tonight?" I couldn't tell if he was fishing himself.

"Need a break from the constant dating whirlwind I'm caught up in," I joked. "And I've got some work to do."

Just then one of his friends stopped by and they talked for a second. It gave me a chance to look Rhys over at close range without seeming obvious. He was cute, in a dangerous sort of way that I couldn't identify but was really drawn to. He said nice things to me . . . sometimes. But I couldn't put my finger on what bugged me. Every time I got close to figuring it out, it was like trying to pin jelly under my thumb.

His friend left and Rhys turned back to me. "No church things to do tonight? Saving the world, converting the masses, smuggling Bibles?" He grinned.

Was he serious? I couldn't tell. "Not tonight. I've already rescued a child from a burning building today. That seemed like enough." I said nothing more for a minute. "Do you have something against Christians?" I finally asked.

"Not at all," he said. "I've just never found any worth talking with . . . till now. They seem very stuck in their own opinions. Kind of like Americans. Always thinking they're right on everything."

"Ah," I said. "Seems like you don't know too many Christians . . . or Americans. Always hard to form an opinion based on a small sample, don't you think?" In my head, I thought, *Of course you don't think. That's why you're on academic probation.* I smiled to myself. And then I blinked, shocked. I didn't mind lighthearted back-and-forth with people, but I had never had many really snarky, *mean* thoughts like that before.

He laughed. "That's what I like about you, Savvy. One thing, anyway. You're not dumb as dirt like a lot of pretty girls."

I gobbled up the compliment and pushed away my chips. "Tell me about Wales," I said, changing the subject. I'd never visited Wales, but after hearing his description, I hoped to someday. "It seems rugged and ancient," I told him. "I appreciate how hard they work to use the Welsh language in spite of English pressing in from every direction."

"Thanks," he said a bit more softly. "I'm sure you'd love it." His phone beeped, and he looked at it and then back at me. "I've got to go; Mum's calling. Maybe next time you can tell me more about your church. Or the U.S. Or both."

He slid out of the booth. After he left, *my* phone beeped. It was a text from Penny.

Do you want me to ask Chloe about Tommy?

How did she know? I hadn't said anything at all to her about Tommy. I texted back innocently.

Tommy?

Don't give me that rubbish, Sav. Do you want me to ask her if they are going out?

I thought about it for a minute. I'd had enough humiliation, and honestly, I wasn't about to be a boy chaser.

No thanks. But I appreciate you asking.

While I finished my Fanta, I read the back of the papers used to wrap my fish-and-chips. Some of it was junk, but the weekly Fish Facts included just for the benefit of the chippies that still wrapped their wares in real newspaper were interesting. This week's happy sample? Puffer Fish.

Puffers come from a family of fish known by various names, including balloonfish, blowfish, and toadies. They are beautifully colored but dangerous to eat, although some people like the thrill. Often after taking the dare to indulge, the unfortunate victim will have a moment when she is lulled into thinking everything is fine. Soon, however, it will be clear something is wrong. Symptoms such as deadening of the tongue and lips, dizziness, and vomiting are followed by numbness and prickling over the body, rapid heart rate, decreased blood pressure, and muscle paralysis. Death finally results from suffocation.

Chapter 22

Saturday. Went to the dog show with Louanne. I tried to talk to her about what was wrong, but she just told me she had to concentrate on Giggle.

Louanne and Growl did exceedingly well.

Didn't see anyone I knew. Especially no one with dark brown hair and Johnny Depp eyes and whom I would find extremely attractive if he weren't already going out with someone.

Rats.

Chapter 23

Monday after school Penny and I hung out in the courtyard so she could say good-bye to Oliver before he left for a football—soccer, to me—match. Then we were going to her house.

Oliver came out of the gym with his uniform on. He stepped to the side to talk to Penny. His teammates razzed him as they all headed toward the bus. I couldn't help but tease Penny, too.

"What? No kiss this time?"

Penny blushed. "It doesn't happen often. I'm actually pretty old-fashioned. My parents wouldn't even let me date until I turned sixteen."

"What?" I blurted. "I'm fifteen—I'll be sixteen in July—and I've never been kissed. I've never even *danced* with a guy if you don't count my dad and my crazy uncle Ed. I'm plenty old-fashioned, too."

She grinned. "Okay. So, if you *were* to dance with someone, who would it be?"

I thought. "Well, I dunno. I had a crush on Jack—but don't tell Melissa, 'cause I don't like him anymore. I normally don't like blonds, so I don't know what that was all about. Probably because he was the editor of the paper."

"Rhys is blond."

"Thank you for helpfully pointing that out." I swung my bag over my shoulder, and we made our way through the courtyard.

"Tommy is a brunet. Prefer them?" she teased. "Opposites attract and all that."

"Is this payback for the kiss comment?" I asked.

"Nope. I am your best friend, though, aren't I? You can't go on pretending you don't like him whilst you really do."

I didn't answer, and I guess in a way that was an answer in itself. Instead I pointed at the ancient, arthritic fingers of wood curling around the arbors leading to her home, Hill House. "Have you noticed that the wisterias are starting to bloom, and their blooms actually look like clusters of juicy grapes?"

Penny said nothing for a minute. "That's lovely, Savvy. It's no wonder you want to be a writer. How do you know so much about flowers?"

"My mother is—was—a great gardener. She loved to garden at our old house. But she hasn't been able to do much here yet."

"My mum is a gardener too," Penny said.

Just then we arrived at Hill House and walked up the long drive to the front door, where two Irish setters enthusiastically bounded out to greet us. For Penny's sake I gritted my teeth and pretended to like the dogs jumping all over me. They were happy, after all. But Louanne was the dog person in our family.

I followed Penny into her kitchen. "Hello, Mrs. Barrowman."

"Well, hullo, Savannah," she replied. Penny's mother was wearing a cashmere sweater set, wool pants, and pearls. I noticed a housekeeper bustling about in the background. "You'll stay for supper tonight, then?"

"Yes, thank you for the invitation," I said. I hoped there wouldn't be lots of strange utensils like oyster forks and fish knives that I had no idea how to use. Didn't want to embarrass Penny.

"Let's go upstairs," Penny said after kissing her mother on the cheek.

I followed her up the long, twisty stairway and into her suite—I mean, room. Once there she threw her book bag in the corner and slipped on her fuzzy slippers. "I found a new quiz for us." She threw a magazine my way. I started making check marks in blue ink—Penny had already answered in red—to see what my conflict style was.

"So did you find a fancy dress?"

"A . . . what?"

"A fancy dress," I said. "You know, for the ball."

She giggled. "Oh, Savvy. *Fancy dress* means a costume. I really couldn't show up at the ball in a costume, right?"

I blushed at my mistake. "Still learning British English," I mumbled.

"I know," she said kindly. "But no, I didn't find anything to wear."

I set down the magazine. "Really? I thought for sure you did but you weren't telling me about it because you didn't want to hurt my feelings."

"Really, I didn't find anything," she said. "The other girls found stuff. Most of the dresses were really cute. Except Chloe's was a little . . . awkward looking."

I crooked my eyebrow at her, and we both laughed. I was sure Chloe's dress looked great. But Penny was a loyal friend. "I went to Be@titude on Friday, and they had great dresses. Do you want to run down there before dinner and check them out?"

"You don't mind?" Penny asked.

"Not at all. We should get there before the best dresses are gone."

Penny leaped up. "Perfect! I had fun with the girls on Friday, but I really missed your advice. You know, a lot of their dresses were kind of uptight, and I'm going for a more, uh, relaxed look now."

She ran downstairs to make sure her mom was fine with our going, and then we took off to the village square. "I've got to drop something off at the post for my mum," she said. We walked into the chemist's shop, which had the post office in the back, and she handed the letter across the counter to the postman.

He looked at me and grinned. "How's the writing coming, Miss Smith?"

I grinned back. "My pen has yet to run out of ink!" I was one of the few people who knew his secret—that he was "Father Christmas" too. I still had the *Times* of London pen he'd delivered to my house on Christmas Day.

A few minutes later Penny and I arrived at Be@titude.

"You're back!" Becky said. "I'm so glad. The dress is still here." She headed over to the rounder, pulled out the Faerie dress, and held it up.

Penny looked at me. "Dress?"

"Not for me." I shook my head. "My friend Penny needs one, though."

"Oh yes, sure," Becky recovered nicely, sliding Faeries back onto the rack. After talking with Penny for a few minutes to get an idea of what kind of style she liked and what kind of shoes she preferred, she ran through the store and gathered up a few dresses, slung them over her arm like puffy bags of multicolored cotton candy, and headed back to the try-on rooms. "Just let me know if you need help!" she called out as Penny disappeared into the room. I sat on one of the chairs outside the try-ons and waited for Penny to appear.

Meanwhile, I had an incoming text. It was Rhys, wanting to know what I was doing. I started texting back.

"Ahem." I heard Penny clear her throat.

"Oh, sorry," I said. "Rhys gets mad if I don't text him back, like, right away." I pushed Send and turned off my phone.

A disconcerted look crossed Penny's face, but it passed quickly. Then she looked down at her dress. "What not to wear?" she asked.

It was a pink confection that made Penny look like Glinda the Good Witch from *The Wizard of Oz*. Definitely a no-go. We both burst into laughter as Penny pretended to have a magic wand. "No fancy dress," I reminded her.

The second dress, a deep purple one, was a bit too mature. "Vampire getup," she said.

The last dress was perfect. Teal blue and shot through with silver, it had a close-fitted sweetheart bodice and ended midcalf with a little Spanish flounce. "One of a kind," Becky said. "No one else will be wearing this one!"

Penny and I looked at each other, and then she turned back to the three-way mirror and spun around before looking at me again. We said it at the same time: "It's perfect!" Then we jumped up and down and squealed like seven-year-olds.

Becky agreed to put it on hold till Penny could come back the next day with her mom and pay for it. "The bill can tot up rather quickly," Becky said.

"Mum can help me pick out some accessories too," Penny said. "I know she was looking forward to shopping together."

On the way out of the shop, Becky caught my arm. "Thanks for bringing in a friend, Savvy. Every little bit helps."

"You're welcome," I said. Penny headed out ahead of me, and before I walked out the door, I glanced back one last time at the Faerie dress.

Chapter 24

We sat at the dinner table with Penny's mother, father, and older brother. Her oldest brother was away at university.

"Tell us a bit about your family and how you got to London," Mrs. Barrowman said.

I shared about my dad's job and how he'd been offered a chance to move here for at least a few years, maybe for good, and that we'd decided as a family it would be a fun adventure.

"And has it?" Penny's brother asked.

"Mostly," I said. "I'm starting to feel like I really fit in here."

"Welcome home," her dad said kindly.

"Her mum likes to garden." Penny turned toward her mother. "Just like you!"

111

"Well, then," Mrs. Barrowman said, "perhaps she'd like to come on the second . . . ?"

I saw Penny catch her mother's eye and shake her head ever so slightly. Mrs. Barrowman let her voice drop and then picked up another topic. "Pudding, anyone?" She stood to clear the dishes. I knew pudding meant all desserts. There was a general murmur of approval. Penny got up to help her mother clear the dishes but indicated that I should stay in my seat.

"You're a guest," she said. I had the feeling, though, that she wanted to talk with her mom in private, in the kitchen.

I sat there, a bit deflated. Had her mother just been about to invite my mom to a gardening event, something my mom would love? It sure seemed like it. So why had Penny shushed her?

I made it through the pudding with a smile fixed to my face, but I was pretty eager to get home. Her dad drove me, and Penny and I made small talk, but I ended up thinking that maybe I had used the wrong fork or something. Or maybe it was my fancy dress mistake.

Did Penny think my mom wouldn't fit in with her mom's upper-class friends?

Did I know Penny as well as I thought I did?

Chapter 25

That night at home, I had to sort through all the potential Asking for Trouble questions. Because they were mostly written by teenage girls, and because I was a teenage girl, I related to most of them. Pretty much every week, though, after praying about it, I figured out which one I was supposed to answer. Then I went to the Source for the answer and wrote it up in my own style. Even though I couldn't actually tell my readers that my answers were from Scripture, I knew I was feeding them good things.

"Fear of the Lord is the foundation of true wisdom. All who obey his commandments will grow in wisdom," I thought. "Psalm 111:10," I said aloud, thankful for the Bible memory program I'd attended as a kid.

I sorted through the questions, and one struck my heart. Not only because I knew it was important to a lot of girls, but also because it was important to me right that very day. If I wrote this advice out and then didn't follow it myself, I would be a hypocrite. Besides, it was the right thing to do. I prayed about it, searched through my online Bible program, and composed the answer. Then I e-mailed it to Jack and gave myself till Friday to follow my own advice.

By Thursday, when I delivered the papers, I still hadn't done it. I didn't have time to read the column before maths, so after Gwennie and Jill and I had finished growing bacteria cultures in science, I sat down and read it.

Dear Asking for Trouble,
I have a problem I hope you can help me with. I'm worried that my best friend has been talking about me behind my back. I never would have guessed it—she's so honest! And trustworthy! Or so I thought. But I heard something through another friend that I think could have only

come from one source: my best friend. What should I do? If I accuse her and I'm wrong, she's going to be mad—and rightly so. But if she's telling tales and spreading my secrets, I should know before I tell her anything else. Right? Help!

Sincerely,
Loose Lips Sink Friendships

Dear Loose Lips,
When you decide that someone is your best friend, you've decided to entrust a lot of your heart, your mind, and your hopes to them. Not to mention your I'll-die-if-anyone-else-knows secrets. So if you have any doubts at all about your friend's trustworthiness, you need to have a chat with her. Now don't go accusing her of anything. (See your letter above!) Just take her aside privately, one-on-one, and tell her what you heard. Ask if you might have misunderstood something, and be humble—see what she says. Nine times out of ten it's a simple misunderstanding, and

you'll be closer than ever. Of course, if it's the other one time out of ten, then you have to be brave enough to kindly say *au revoir, adios, sayonara,* or however you like to politely say good-bye.

Sincerely,
We're All in the Same Boat

At lunch I asked Penny if we could walk in the courtyard and talk.

Once we were out there, she asked, "What's up?"

"Well, I know this is the dumbest thing ever, and I'm an insecure bowl of jelly, but I was just wondering about something. You know when your mom was ready to ask about my mom and some gardening thing, the other night at dinner?"

Penny nodded.

"Well, I was just wondering. Are we not, you know, high class enough for you?"

Penny looked at me as if I'd just swallowed a live bug and asked for another with a splash of soy sauce. "Pardon?"

"I was just wondering why you stopped her, was all." I hung my head.

Penny grabbed my arm and sat me down on one of the benches. "Even though some others might feel differently, I don't think, in any way, that I am any better than you—or that my family is either. The party my mum was going to bring up is for the day after the May Day Ball. Traditionally, all my friends and their mums go over to one of the gardens—Ashley's house was last year—and the girls serve tea and cakes to the mums while they look at the newest blooms and plan garden meetings for the year. Members are allowed to nominate new people for membership, and voting happens in May."

"Oh," I said, still not getting why my mom couldn't be invited.

"Everyone wears their May Day Ball gown from the night before," Penny said. "It's a way for the mums to ooh and aah over everyone's dress. If you still want to come, you could wear something nice . . ."

Now I got it. "No, it'd feel kind of awkward," I said.

"I thought so," Penny said. She squeezed my arm as we got up. "You're a fantastic friend, Savvy. I'm so glad you moved here. I'd never leave you out if I thought it would hurt you."

And with that, we headed back to lunch. Silently, I prayed that whoever had written to the Asking for Trouble column had had as good of an outcome with her friend.

As I was leaving the lunchroom, Rhys was coming in. "Just who I wanted to see," he said. "Did you have your April Fools thing yet?"

"Next week," I said. "On the day before April Fools'."

"Text me when and where." He took my hand like he owned it and then wrote his name on it in ink. "To remind you." Right before I pulled my hand away, a crush of new people headed into the lunchroom. I'd recognize Chloe's laugh anywhere. Tommy's, too. Tommy and I locked eyes, only for a minute. Rhys looked at him too before making a show of closing his hand around my own.

Chapter 26

Even though I'd spent the last week being a nervous Nellie, on the actual day itself, March 31, I wasn't as worried as I'd thought I would be. Surprisingly, Mom had let me stay home from school to practice—and to pray—and I felt more at peace than I had for a while. Mom was going to a book club meeting with our next-door neighbor Vivienne, so she was going to have to drop me off at church a little early. I'd called Jenny, and she'd promised it would be okay. I could hang out in the youth room and practice and do homework till everyone else arrived.

Outfit? Skinny jeans; blue tank top with country-ish blue, green, and black checked overshirt; new UGGs; silver hoop earrings—not too big an O.

About an hour before we were going to leave, I heard a knock on the door. I opened it with one hand and held my guitar in the other. "Hello," I said politely.

Vivienne eyed my guitar. From her look, I suspected she'd been listening to me practice all day. She wasn't a fan, but I couldn't help it. I'd tried to keep it low. "This is for your mum," she said, handing over a canvas tote bag with that evening's books. "Tell her we'll have to leave promptly."

With another withering look at the guitar, she waved toodle-loo and headed back toward her house. I have to admit, my confidence wavered, but only for a moment.

"Ready to go, Sav?" Mom asked. "And are you sure Dad can't come by tonight to listen? I could even skip the book club if you want me to. And Louanne could come."

I shook my head. "Nope. Only youth group people allowed. Otherwise we wouldn't be willing to be fools," I said. And it was true. I really didn't want to make a fool of myself in front of my parents and Louanne. It should have been just the opposite—they loved me the most and would judge me the least if I failed. But their opinion also mattered the most, and I wanted to be just right in their eyes.

The ride there was silent. Maybe I was more nervous than I'd thought.

"Rhys said he might come," I finally said.

"Oh," Mom replied.

"Aren't you excited that he could come and hear the gospel?"

"I'm happy anytime someone hears the gospel," she nonanswered.

"How can you not like him? You don't even know him!"

"Mother's intuition, Savvy," she said. "And the effect he has on you."

"What effect? You're imagining things." As soon as I said the words, I realized how uncharacteristic they were of me. And harsh. "Sorry," I said. But I didn't look at her.

She pulled in front of the church and took my hand in hers. "Lord, I pray that You'll be with Savvy tonight. Steady her hands and her voice, and help her to remember every note she's so faithfully practiced. Bless her as she seeks to bless others in Your name. Amen."

"Thank you, Mom." I got out of the car and opened the back door, taking my guitar and my

WA *Times* notebook. I'd brought some home-work and next week's AFT questions to work on while I waited for the others to arrive for practice.

I lugged it all into the back of the youth room, set down my guitar, and spread out my notebook and papers on a small desk near the back. I would work on the Asking for Trouble questions first—looking up the answers at church seemed like a good idea. Then homework. I started reading through the questions and then noticed that the donation boxes were already set up nearby.

That first night, before Joe had asked me if I'd like to participate, I'd promised Supriya that I'd donate my funds to her, and I meant to keep that promise. But so it wouldn't look funny, maybe I'd just put them in now, before anyone else came. I stood up and took my three bills—two ten-pound notes and a five-pound note—and slipped them into her box.

Please help Be@titude some way too, Lord, I prayed. I actually did want to win, but I didn't want to say that, even in my prayer. When I turned around, people were filtering into the room. I headed back to the desk, scooped up the papers, and set them with my open notebook in an untidy heap on the floor underneath my box.

I grabbed my guitar and looked at the clock. It was almost time.

Chapter 27

"So is everyone ready, then?" Joe gathered us all into a small room off the main youth area. I could smell the coffee brewing on the barista cart, but I didn't dare have any caffeine before playing. Didn't want my hands or my voice to shake.

"I'm ready," a kid named Jacob said. He could juggle up to seven balls at once and was going on first to get everyone pumped up.

We prayed together and then filtered to the back of the room so we'd be able to enjoy watching the other performances while waiting to do our own thing. Juggling Jacob went first and, as promised, got everyone worked up and hooting and clapping. I watched him and clapped, but I had to admit that I had at least one eye on the door most of the time.

"Who are you looking for?" Supriya asked.

I shook my head and whispered, "I'll tell you later." Part of me hoped that Rhys would come because it'd be good for him to hear the message at the end and also to get a better picture of the Christians he liked to put down.

Next up was a group of guys lip-synching. Then someone played a piano song to chill everyone out before a few slower acts came on.

Just as Supriya was about to take the stage and recite in her beautiful, exotic-sounding Hindi, I glanced back at the door.

"He's here," Supriya whispered.

He was here all right. But it wasn't the *he* I'd expected.

It was Tommy. *Oh no!*

I looked away so I wouldn't have to catch his eye as he made his way through the crowd toward his friends. I tried really hard to listen to Supriya's poem, I really did, but it was hard to focus. I asked the Lord to calm my shaking hands. And then it was my turn to go on stage.

Chapter 28

Joe introduced me from the stage and asked me to tell a little bit about my charity.

"I chose Be@titude." My voice was shaky at first, but it smoothed out as I warmed up to the topic. "The shop is in Wexburg, where I—where some of us in this church—are from." At that I involuntarily glanced at Tommy. "Anyway, she's trying to help single mothers get back to work at something they enjoy so they can support their families. The Lord has always been about helping those who need it, and I thought it'd be a good ministry to support."

I took just a second to tune my guitar. "Anyway, here's my song. It's by an American singer and songwriter, Taylor Swift. I think it's cool that she's not much older than me and writes her own music. She writes about things we can relate to." I kept my voice very even here, betraying nothing, I hoped.

"The song has a number of different meanings for me. I hope you enjoy it."

I started to play and sing, and I lost myself in the words—and the double entendre known, I hoped, only to the Lord and to me.

I didn't snap out of the zone till I sang the very last words in the song:

> *"Have you ever thought just maybe*
> *You belong with me."*

The crowd applauded loudly, and I heard one whistle. I smiled and bowed and met Supriya's supportive gaze. Then I headed off the stage, guitar in hand, to the back room.

Chapter 29

Sunday morning I sat in church, trying to focus on the words the pastor was speaking from 2 Corinthians and not be distracted by the kid in front of me who was picking his ear and then eating the harvest. In order to keep my mind off him, I started to doodle on the back of my bulletin. I was nothing like Penny in drawing, I knew. But it kept my mind busy.

"So what does the Lord mean when He says, 'Do not be yoked together with unbelievers'?" Pastor said. "No sharing eggs with heathens?" We all laughed.

"Does that mean we shouldn't have friends who are not Christians? By no means. We are to show God's love to those who do not understand it, to invite them into an understanding, to do good deeds for them so that our Father may be glorified. Jesus showed us the way. He befriended many, but those with whom He shared His heart— His closest friends—were believers."

Pastor coughed a little and took a drink of water before continuing. The kid ahead of me had fallen asleep and was now leaning on his mom's shoulder, so it was safe for me to look up again as Pastor finished talking. "According to this passage, we do not unite that which is sacred with something that is not. Your heart, your body as the temple of the Holy Spirit, your soul, your work and ministries—all are sacred."

As he was asking us to bow our heads again and pray, I looked down at my drawing. My sumo cows didn't look like they had a yoke on them. Rather, one looked like it was strangling the other.

After the service, I grabbed a coffee before heading to the youth group room. Supriya was hanging in the coffee lounge too. On the way to Sunday school, I asked her, "So what did you think of the sermon?"

"It was good. You?"

I nodded. "Back in the States our youth pastor

had talked about not dating non-Christians. It's funny that in a way he was basically saying the same thing here too." I crunched my coffee cup and made a perfect rimmer into a nearby garbage can. Supriya laughed.

"What are you laughing at?"

"You," she teased. "Of course the pastor is going to say the same thing here, Sav. The Bible is the same here as it is there. It's the same everywhere."

I blushed a little—*thinkpink*—admitting with my coloring that I'd just had a *duh* moment.

The crowd in Sunday school was really thick, and we pretty much stayed close to the door rather than pushing our way through the pack. I closed my eyes, mostly, during worship. I did notice one time when I opened them that Tommy was there lifting his hands in praise.

He belongs to someone else, Sav, I reminded myself. *Just like Jack and Melissa and Brian and Hazelle. I'm a girl with ethics. Move on.*

Chapter 30

Later that night Louanne was still moping around. She'd been faithfully collecting my copies of the Wexburg Academy *Times*, and I was starting to worry that she was developing a hoarding disorder.

"Are you sure you're okay?" I asked her. "I mean, that's what big sisters are for, you know. To help." *Wish I had a big sister*, I thought. I was on my own. "Want to talk about the dog show? I could take some new pictures of Growl—Giggle."

She shook her head, went to the bathroom, got a tissue, and blew her nose. I noticed she had a couple of tiny, veiny scratches on the back of her right hand. She saw me looking at them and put her hand into her pocket.

"Want to play a game, then?" I asked. "Monop-oly? Scrabble?"

She looked up. "Scrabble would be okay."

"Good!" I reached into the armoire below the telly—it was still on and blaring *Top Gear*—and pulled out our Scrabble board. "You can even go first," I said.

I dumped all our tiles into a bucket—we had combined three games' worth so we'd have lots of letters—and then we each chose our stack and spread them across our racks. Louanne spelled her first word across the red star in the middle. *W-O-R-R-Y.*

"Good job!" I said. "Lots of points there."

She smiled and drew five replacement tiles while I puzzled out my word. *W-R-O-N-G,* I spelled down from her *W.*

F-E-A-R was her next play, using one of the *R*s in *WORRY.*

Y-O-K-E-D, I put down. A sense of dread began to steal across the room as twilight fell.

Louanne played *D-I-E-* and then looked at me. "Are you having fun, Savvy?"

"Sure . . ." I looked her in the eye, a little shocked at her last word. "Well, not really."

"Me neither," she said, upending the board. "Let's play another time, okay?"

Just then my phone beeped. I had a text message. From Rhys. "Sure," I answered my sister before looking at the text. "Ice cream in half an hour?"

Louanne nodded, and I left, taking my phone with me. The room seemed brighter, and my head was a little light. Rhys hadn't contacted me for a long time. What could he want?

Do you have time to talk? I could call you.

My fingertips tingled as they hung over the dial pad for a minute before I texted back.

Okay.

I headed upstairs and barely made it into my room before the phone rang.

Chapter 31

"Hi," I said, shutting my door.

"So I was just checking in," he said.

Rhys never just checked in.

"I'm fine."

I was trying to think of small talk to lighten things up. Talking on the phone seemed way more serious than texting. "Just getting ready to work on science. We're culturing bacteria."

He laughed, but his laugh had a sharp edge. "So appropriate. Reminds me of a lot of people at this school. Bacteria is the only culture they have."

I didn't say anything.

His voice softened. "How was your April Fools thing the other night? I'm sorry I couldn't make it."

I noticed he didn't say why, and I didn't ask.

"It was good," I said. "I think we raised a lot of money for good organizations."

"Was anyone a fool?" His voice had a hint of sarcasm to it. I wasn't sure if he was referring to my faith, but in case he was, I thought I'd address it right away.

"Not that I know of," I said. "But I don't mind being a fool for Christ."

"I like that about you, Savvy. You're different—you're strong. Which is why I'm calling you. I was wondering, well . . . do you have a date for the May Day Ball yet? And if not, would you consider going with me?"

I sat there waiting for a few seconds before finally speaking up. "Wow, Rhys, I'm really surprised. Surprised you don't already have a date . . . and surprised you'd ask *me*."

"I could have asked other people, Savvy—I still could. But you're my first choice. I like you . . . a lot. Think about it for a few days. And then let me know, because it's getting pretty close and I can't wait forever, all right?"

"Right," I agreed. That seemed fair. I wondered who else he could ask. Who else wasn't going? It didn't really matter. What mattered was . . . did I want to go with him?

"I'd best get going. Got loads of homework to do," he said, laughing lightly. "I'm sure you do too."

"Okay. Talk to you soon," I said.

"I'm hoping so." Then he clicked off.

I just sat there on my floor. Did I want to go with him? There was nothing wrong with going as friends, right? Yeah, there might have been a little bit of a draw toward more—one I didn't necessarily want but couldn't get rid of. But I was pretty confident I could keep things at "just friends." I was sure he'd totally understand that, and he probably only thought of me as a friend too, which is what would make it fine.

But were we actually friends?

Maybe not exactly . . . but I felt like we probably *could* be. Besides, I knew he wasn't really my type, but there was a little thrill when I was with him because I never knew what he was going to do or say next. He was nice looking. A little dangerous, maybe. And other girls envied me.

I shook my head to clear my thoughts and texted Penny. Maybe she'd have an idea of what to do.

Hey, Penny. What's up?

A few minutes later my phone vibrated.

Can't text now, with Mum. Check this out, though!

A minute later I got a picture message of the beautiful teal dress with silver strappy shoes and a pair of dewdrop earrings.

So, so pretty. I was kind of happy she was too busy to answer.

I didn't text Supriya.

Chapter 32

I headed downstairs to eat some ice cream with Louanne only to find that she'd already gone to bed. I scooped a bowl of chocolate brownie delight for myself and took it back to my room. *Might as well look at some of the Asking for Trouble letters*, I thought. *And tidy up a few things to give to Natalie tomorrow.*

I'd put together a big packet of information on Be@titude, profiling one of the moms they'd helped. I also looked up the history of May Day, staying away from the Communist implications, as I'd been warned to stay away from politics. I also ignored all the pagan junk. Instead, I focused on the celebration of spring—and new life—after a long, wet winter. And the Maydayrun motorbike race that took place every year. Big bikes, fabbo helmets, loud engines, and speed. I wouldn't mind seeing it someday.

I logged into my e-mail system. Wow! There were about ten letters to choose from this week. I quickly scanned the subject lines and then the senders' addresses. I always wondered if Ashley or Penny or even Hazelle would ever send a letter.

What? I enlarged my screen to 125 percent. I couldn't believe my eyes. But there it was.

A letter from my sister—Louanne! I clicked it open.

Dear Asking for Trouble,

I have a big problem and I don't know what to do. It's not dangerus, but it could be a bigger problem really soon. My family is nice, but if I tell anyone, they'll make me do something I really can't do and then I would have to disobey and get in even more trouble. What should I do?

Was she in trouble? Should I confront her? She said it wasn't dangerous, but still . . .

I stayed up late and prayed about it, and I looked up Scripture to write my answer. Then

I mailed in my response to Jack. Would he be surprised to see it a day early?

I'll answer her question in this week's paper. If I don't see an improvement in a week, or ten days at the most, I'll confront her and tell Mom and Dad.

Growl scratched at my door, which was odd. Normally he was glued to Louanne, even while she was sleeping.

Chapter 33

I got to school early the next day. Good thing, too, because if Penny was the good witch Glinda, then Natalie was the Wicked Witch of the West, and she was waiting for me in the WA *Times* office.

"I'm not sure if this is all you could come up with, Savannah," she said, throwing a sheaf of papers at me, "but mostly it's rubbish. You just focused your attention on your friends as couples, your pet project clothing store, and some happy-go-lucky nonfacts about May Day. Care to try again?"

I suddenly had a new understanding of the wounds caused by a *paper cut*.

Everyone in the office kept their heads down—listening, I knew, but not intervening. "No, actually, I don't," I said. "I've done my best, and if this won't work, I'm sorry, but I won't be a help to you on this article." I was sorry Melissa would be let down. Neither she nor Jack was there that morning.

"Fine, then," Natalie said. "Since you clearly can't follow directions, I'll take the snaps at the ball myself."

I nodded but said nothing so as not to betray the sorrow caught in my throat. Just peachy. Why did she have to come back? I headed toward the back and asked Rob if I could use his computer for a minute. "Sure, Savvy," he said. "Sorry about Little Miss Sunshine. You could always talk to the adviser about her."

I shook my head. I had my secret assignment. I had friends on staff. I'd make my own way in my own time.

"I'm off to class, then," he said. "Log off when you're done, all right?"

"Okay." I logged on to my e-mail to see that Jack had already confirmed receipt of my column and had forwarded a few new messages to me. I quickly looked through them to see if there was anything new from Louanne. Mostly just the usual suspects—boy trouble, friend trouble, parent trouble. One caught my eye. The subject line simply said, *I Know.*

I read it quickly, one eye on the clock, knowing that Mr. Thompson was going to come down hard on me if I was late again.

> Hullo. I have a few of your papers—rough drafts of questions and answers that let me know your real identity as the author of the Asking for Trouble column. I've kept it a secret. Do you want your papers back, or should I destroy them?

Someone knew my secret! But who? And how?

I logged off and then raced to class, sliding into my seat just as the bell stopped ringing. I didn't offer Brian gum, and I didn't look at Hazelle to see if she had any sympathy at all for me after my interaction with Natalie that morning. I pretended to jot down what Mr. Thompson was saying, but my entire brain was focused on one question: *Who knows?*

Could it be Hazelle? or Rob or Rodney or Melissa? Someone at the paper was the most likely choice because they could have stumbled upon something in the newspaper office. But no one had given the tiniest hint.

Who else? Louanne . . . from last night's e-mail?

Possibly. But the e-mail voice was pretty mature. And Louanne would have said, *hi* or *hello* and not *hullo* like most Brits.

Where had I kept those papers? In my notebook. And where had I taken my notebook? Everywhere.

I worried about it all day. On my way out of school I bumped into Rhys, who happened to be standing near the exit I normally took on my way home.

"Hey, Savannah." He looked at my face. "You okay?"

I took a deep breath. "I guess so."

"Can I help?" He really did seem concerned. "Do I need to step in and break some skulls for you?"

I smiled but wasn't sure if he really meant it or not. "I assume you don't beat up girls," I said back. Since he'd appeared really concerned, and since one of the deals had gone down in a public newsroom, I decided to just say, "Well, I had a major disagreement with someone on the newspaper staff today. I was supposed to be a partner and the photographer for the May Day Ball article. But Natalie took me off—and told me off—in front of everyone."

He rested his arm on my shoulder. I could smell the rosemary mint of his shampoo. It wasn't unpleasant, but it was hard to breathe with him this close. "I'm sorry. But maybe it'll all work out for the best. Even if she was mean. It might make it possible for you to enjoy the ball yourself."

I nodded. I was aware that I hadn't answered him and that I needed to so he could ask someone else if he wanted to. "I've got to chat with my mother tonight," I said. "And then I'll let you know after school tomorrow. Okay?"

He stood back and smiled. "Take my picture to show your mum."

My first thought was, *Wow, a little overconfident?* But then he made a crazy face and it made me laugh. I took a pic with my phone and headed home to talk with my mom.

I had noticed that he'd kept a complete poker face when I'd mentioned the paper. But Rhys would. I got the feeling he never let anyone know what I was truly feeling.

Chapter 34

"So why aren't you saying anything?" I asked my mom as she stared at the picture of Rhys.

"I'm looking," Mom answered.

"Is it the ponytail? Because it's really short and neat. All those guys in the Bible wore long hair. And so did the guys in the American Revolution."

My mother looked up and rolled her eyes at me. "And so did your father for a time, and I obviously don't think he's a bad guy."

"He did?" I couldn't believe it. "Dad?"

She nodded. "Dad."

"And look at him. Could he be nicer? cleaner? healthier? The man drinks tomato juice for breakfast every day."

Mom patted the couch beside her. "Sav, it's not the ponytail. It's just that every time you talk about this boy, you're not yourself. You're either really up or really down or really confused. You don't know what he thinks or what he believes or what you have in common."

"We're friends," I insisted. "So we'd only be going as friends."

"Friends talk about issues; they help each other; they feel comfortable with each other. I don't know your heart, but from my point of view, that doesn't seem to be happening here. And does *he* know you're just friends?"

I tapped my foot for a minute. Then I took off my shoes and tossed them into the corner, scaring Growl. That hadn't even been my intention—this time. *That dog is as dumb as dirt*, I thought. Then I looked up. Why had I thought *that*?

"I am sure he does."

My mother looked doubtful.

"I'll tell him in very straight words," I promised. "Can I go?"

"This has to be your decision, Savvy," she said. "But I want you to think hard about it. When you go out with someone, dress up, or even just become friends with him, you are giving away a precious piece of yourself. Make sure that each person you give a piece of Savvy to deserves it."

I leaned into her arm. "I will, Mom."

She reached her arm around me and stroked my hair. "Firsts are especially important, things you'll always remember. First dances, first formal dresses . . . first kisses . . ."

"I am *not* going to kiss Rhys," I said.

She stood up. "But he may try to kiss you." She ruffled my hair and then padded into the kitchen to do the dishes while I went upstairs to text Penny. I wanted to tell her but didn't actually want to talk with her.

I've decided to go to the May Day Ball with Rhys.

Her answer came right back.

Are you sure, Sav?

Yes. And we're just friends. I'll tell him that.

As long as you're sure that's what you want. . . .
So can my mum invite your mum to the Day After
Garden and Tea Party?

I texted back yes immediately. I didn't tell her, of course, but that was one of my main reasons for wanting to go. There were lots of good reasons to go, of course. To have fun with everyone. To enjoy dancing. To dress up in a formal! And to hang out with Rhys for the night too.

Only one little thing I wasn't looking forward to. Seeing Tommy and Chloe in her I'm-sure-it's-not-awkward dress.

On my way downstairs I stopped by Louanne's room. She was lying on her bed doing her homework. She wasn't exactly beaming with joy, but she looked a little more chipper than she had for a few days.

"Everything okay?" I asked.

"Mmm-hmm," she replied.

"I'll bring a paper home for you on Thursday."

At that, she smiled. "Thanks, Savvy."

I hoped she'd thank me later when she saw my advice.

Then I headed down the creaking steps for a snack and to share the good news with my mother, who was getting caught up on her reading while Dad worked late.

"I have good news," I said.

She set her book down on the sofa beside her. "Do tell!" she teased.

"Well, Penny's mother belongs to this really swish

garden club," I said. "Lots of fancy people, but nice ones too, like Penny's mum. Anyway, they have a garden party and tea the day after the May Day Ball. The mums come and discuss gardening and the girls all show up in their fancy—I mean *formal*—dresses and serve them. And you're going to be invited."

"Me?" Mom said. "Really?"

"Really," I said. "And here's the best part. One of the members can suggest you for membership, and if you're voted in, you can join their club. You can tour the castle and manor gardens with them and everything."

"Oh, that would be fantastic!" Mom snapped her book shut and leaped off the sofa. Next thing I knew, she was browsing and *mmm-hmm*ing titles on the bookshelf next to the telly.

"What are you doing?"

"Looking for my garden books. I need to brush up on my Latin plant names!" She pulled a volume off the shelf and cracked it open. When I left her she was happily muttering, "*Dellis hortensis, Hyacinthus elatus.*"

I grinned. It made me happy to make her elated, er, *elatus*.

Chapter 35

On Wednesday Penny had a dentist appointment at lunch and I felt like sitting by myself in the courtyard. It was so, so beautiful out. The sun gleamed down from on high, and I felt its rays spread across my skin like Icy Hot all the way to my bones. I tilted my head toward the sun, hoping to lure those rays to my face.

Faceus the sunflowerus, I thought and laughed out loud.

"What's so funny? Care to share?"

I sat straight up and opened my eyes, trying to focus a little. "Oh, hey, Tommy." I hoped my hair wasn't splayed all over the place. "Nothing funny. I'm just happy. It's sunny and I love England and I'm full of joy and it's a beautiful day."

Why did all that come out? I had just shared my heart with him. And he'd only asked me a simple question. I hoped he didn't think I was, as the Brits said, "barking mad."

He smiled at me. "Paper coming out tomorrow, eh?"

I nodded. It really was nice of him to remember that.

"I thought you did a great job on the Taylor Swift song at church. I'm glad I made it in enough time to hear you."

"Were you at soccer—I mean, football?" I asked.

"Yep. I also invited a couple of people from school to come. But Bill was playing an away game, and Chloe and Maddie had too much homework."

Ah. Must be their double dates. Tommy and Chloe, Bill and Maddie.

The passing bell rang, and I knew I had to hurry to literature and he was on his way to lunch. I stood and ran my hands through my hair so I'd be presentable in class.

"See you around," I said, distancing myself.

"Keep that joy," he said and headed into second lunch. Chloe was probably already there.

Rhys, too.

Chapter 36

I'd told Rhys that I'd meet him at Fishcoteque after school. He was there. But so was one of his mates. It seemed a little odd, but maybe his friend had already been there when he arrived.

I got a Fanta from Jeannie, who didn't seem quite as cheery again that day. It bothered me, but I shrugged it off. Rhys's friend disappeared back to the dart zone as soon as he saw me heading toward the booth. Rhys scooted over on his side of the booth, but I slid in across the table from him instead.

"How's your day going?" he asked. "No more run-ins with Nasty Natalie?"

I grinned at the nickname. "Nope. She stays on her side of the ring, and I stay on mine."

159

Rhys laughed. "I can't imagine you boxing. You're too *nice*." The way he said it, it didn't exactly sound like a wholehearted compliment. But I wasn't going to be paranoid about it.

He sat across from me, silent, and I fiddled with the napkin, silent too. I had to admit, a certain part of me enjoyed the power of saying nothing when I knew he was expecting me to talk. For once I had the upper hand between us. Which was an odd thought, actually. I jumped right in.

"Thank you so much for inviting me to the May Day Ball," I started out. "I'd really like to go, and I think we'd have a lot of fun as *friends*." I emphasized the word *friends*.

"That's great, Savvy," he said. "I think we'll have a great time. We can split the limo four ways with Ian—" he jerked his thumb toward the dart area, where his friend was playing—"and his date. I can let you know the cost later."

Good. I liked that. Even though it would cost me more money if we were splitting the bill, it would seem more friendlike and less datelike. "Sounds good. Text me the total, and I'll talk to my parents."

"Maybe we could meet each other's parents?" he suggested. "Have dinner together?"

"I don't think we need to," I said. "My parents haven't met all of my *friends here*. And certainly not their parents." Except for Penny, of course, but she was my best friend. "They'll meet you when you come to pick me up."

"Okay. I just thought they might want to, you know, get to know me a little better. Since we'll be, uh, closer . . . *friends*."

"No need," I said.

"Oh, hey. Just a minute." He waved Ian over and asked him for his phone. "I'm going to punch your number into Ian's phone. My mum took mine earlier this week after I, well, uh, never mind why. But if you need me, text Ian. And if I need you, I'll text you from Ian's phone."

Wow. He really wanted to make sure he could stay in touch with me at all times.

We chatted for a few minutes, with him well at ease and me ill at ease, and then I said I'd better head home. A thick fog capped the day as I rounded the corner of Cinnamon Street toward the warm glow of Kew Cottage.

Mom was cooking as I walked into the kitchen. I noticed a book on the counter. She peeked at it as she stirred whatever was on the stovetop.

I glanced at the cover of the book as I headed to the fridge for a snack.

"Good day?" she asked.

"Yep!"

"Good! I have a great idea. On Saturday let's go to that shop you've been talking about—Be@titude—and see if we can find you a great dress and some shoes."

That perked me up. "Sounds great!" I dug around in the fridge till I found a jar of mandarin orange slices to take upstairs to my room. Once there, I sat on the floor with my jar and a fork and my guitar.

I looked at the music for a while, trying to decide what to practice next. I forked a few mandarin oranges till I realized how much the chubby slices looked like the koi in Aunt Tricia's backyard pond. I was no fanatic like Louanne, but even I couldn't eat them after that.

I opened the music. One title definitely caught my eye. "You Don't Have to Call Me." Why hadn't I spoken up and said I didn't want Ian to have my number?

Too *nice*, maybe.

Chapter 37

Thursday afternoon I came right home and *thwapped* that day's Wexburg Academy *Times* down in front of Louanne, who was in the kitchen once again. "Here you go," I said. "Practically ran home, as I promised I would."

"Thanks, Savvy." She gave me the first genuine smile I'd seen in a long time. But she wouldn't open the paper before I left the kitchen. I peeked in from the living room and noticed Louanne moving toward the back door.

Dear Asking for Trouble,
I have a big problem and I don't know what to do. It's not dangerus, but it could be a bigger problem really soon.

My family is nice, but if I tell anyone, they'll make me do something I really can't do and then I would have to disobey and get in even more trouble. What should I do?

Dear Dangerus,
It's really hard to have a big problem and keep it all to yourself. Sometimes there are ideas or solutions you can't see that someone else can. That's why it's always wise to get a few opinions or help from other people when trying to solve your problems. Why don't you ask someone with the same values as you to help you out? That way they won't ask you to do something you really can't do, and you won't have to disobey, either. Give yourself no more than one week to figure out who that might be. I can assure you that asking for help is better than asking for trouble.

Trustworthily Yours,
Asking for Trouble

Today was Thursday. I'd give her till Saturday the seventeenth, a week plus one day's grace, and if she hadn't spoken up by then, I'd have to break my own code of silence and let her know who I was.

Of course, someone else already knew who I was. I was toying with the idea of e-mailing them back, but I wondered if ignoring it altogether was a better strategy. I had to figure it out before someone else did. Like Natalie.

Chapter 38

Saturday afternoon was rainy, but Mom and I decided to walk to Be@titude anyway and make a day of it. We huddled together under a large brolly, giggling as we made our way up Cinnamon Street. Several others recognized us by now and waved in a friendly manner.

"Bit damp—can't let it get the best of us then, right?" one plump neighbor lady said as her broom *tsk-tsked* correctingly across her damp sidewalk, brushing cigarette butts, soppy leaves, and a stray piece of paper into an obedient pile.

"Of course not!" Mom called back with a cheery wave. I think we'd earned some respect points by not letting the wet get to us.

167

"Let's have tea beforehand," Mom offered. Never one to turn down a snack, I agreed.

We walked up to the Orange Pekoe, and Mom shook and closed the umbrella before we walked in. A matronly woman with a white apron as wide as her smile greeted us. "Drop your brollies in the bucket, please!" she said before seating us at a cozy table near the window. She handed a tea menu to each of us—yes, a whole menu with only tea selections on it. I ordered blackberry bramble, and Mom ordered queen's choice. A few minutes later, our waitress came by and set two plump white pots on the table along with charmingly chipped white china cups. Right in the middle of our table she gently set down a three-tiered tray with plates of treats on it.

"Lower tray you'll find your sandwiches and such," she said. "Do try the watercress. It's particularly lovely today." She then pointed out the middle layer. "Here are the hot items. Youse might want to try them first. Crab cakes, a little quiche. Mistress Brown in the back prides herself on the quiche." She then indicated the smallish plate on top. "The sweets, of course. Little pot of sticky toffee pudding. Our homemade biscuits. And chocolate custard. Our specialty."

She toddled back to the kitchen, and Mom

and I started in on our food and tea. "Are you excited?" she asked me.

"About the tea?"

"About the dance, silly. And the dress."

"I am *so* excited about the dress, Mom. I only hope she still has the one I like. Although . . . I don't know how much it costs." I had some money saved, but I was going to need help from Mom and Dad. I was well aware that this whole deal was going to cost a bundle. Dress, shoes, ball tickets, splitting the limo. Rhys had insisted on paying for my dinner. I had reluctantly agreed.

"And how about Rhys?" Mom asked. "Is he excited?"

I didn't want to tell her that I thought it unlikely he got excited about anything because she'd like him even less than she did now. But I also didn't like keeping secrets from my mom. Louanne had a secret. It wasn't a good thing. Was mine? "I think he's really looking forward to it," I said. I popped a crab cake into my mouth and then ate some pudding and tried a watercress sandwich even though I was full to bursting. If I kept eating, I didn't have to talk.

Mom didn't seem to mind. She was going on about all the flowers she'd seen on her latest excursion to a huge garden centre the day she drove Dad to work so she could take the car. "The things I could do if I had that whole back garden," she said. "It wouldn't be big like your friends' gardens," she mused. "But I'd think of a theme."

Just as we were about to pay, I heard an argument starting a few tables behind me. By nature or culture, British people have soft, controlled voices, especially in public. So a loud disagreement would certainly be considered bad form.

"So rude," Mom said. "She looks to be about your age, and she's treating her mother terribly."

I could hear some of the things being said, and they sure didn't sound kind. I couldn't help it. Even though I didn't have my notebook (in fact, I left it home more often now), my journalist's sensibilities got the best of me. I had to see who that was.

"I'm going to the loo," I said. "Before we shop."

As I stood up, I purposely dropped my purse on the floor so I could turn around to see who it was. She didn't seem to recognize me, but I recognized her.

Chloe.

Chapter 39

As we walked into Be@titude, the door chimes twinkled a merry hello. Becky was helping a customer and there was another one in line, but she gave me a little wave to show she'd be right with me. It felt really grown-up, actually, having the store owner recognize me.

"Over here," I said to Mom. I headed to the rack where the tea green dress had been a few weeks back when I'd been here with Penny. As I looked through the rack for my size, the dresses were so thick and some so puffy that they crushed into each other. At first glance, I couldn't find the one I was looking for. "Maybe it's pressed between some of the other dresses," I said. I went through every dress in that size. Nothing.

"It's gone," I said. I just knew it. Truthfully, I would have been surprised if such a great dress had still been there.

"Let's look in the other sizes," Mom said. "If there's a larger one, we could have it taken in."

I shook my head. "Nope. Becky only buys one of each style. She told me herself." I looked up and Becky caught my eye, smiled, and turned her attention to the woman she was helping. The first customer had already completed her purchase, so I knew I was next.

"There have to be some other beauties," Mom said. She held up a yellow gossamer number.

"Mom, I'd look like Rapunzel in that," I said. "Yellow washes me out."

"This?"

I grimaced. Lavender was fine for flowers, but not for a gown. I finally found one in deep red that might work. It looked more fall than spring, but hey, beggars couldn't be choosers, right? This was what came of waiting till the last minute. Not that I could help it.

Becky walked over. "Hullo, Savvy. Thanks for waiting. This must be your mum?"

Mom held out her hand. "So pleased to meet

you. Savvy's told me all about you and your ministry here."

Becky grinned. "You're raising a top journalist," she said. "I fully expect to see her byline in the *Times* of London someday."

"I hope to see it in the *Times* of Wexburg Academy first," I teased. "So would you help me find a dress?" I tried to keep the disappointment over the loss of the tea green gown out of my voice.

"Going to the May Day Ball after all, then?"

I nodded. I knew I wasn't beaming, but I was pleased.

"I might have something in the back," she said. Mom and I looked at shoes while we waited. A few minutes later she swished out of the back with a dress in a clear plastic bag.

"Faeries!" I squealed. "That's it, Mom; that's it!"

Becky laughed out loud. "I just had a feeling that you'd end up at the May Day Ball. I set it in the back figuring I'd sell it during wedding season if not now. But I'm very glad it's going home with its rightful owner." She held the hanger out to me, and I dashed toward the try-on rooms in the back.

I wriggled out of my jeans and sweater and slipped the gown over my head. It fell . . . perfectly. It fit me in all the right places, neither too tight nor too loose. It brought out the natural highlights in my hair. I wouldn't need to wear high heels to pull it off—and giraffe over Rhys, who was the same height as me.

I stepped out of the changing room and onto the showroom floor, debuting the dress in my anklets and no shoes.

"Oh, Savvy, that is perfect," Mom said. "It's exactly you."

I twirled a little for effect—something I hadn't done since I'd tried out for the baton-twirling team as a kid.

"Shall I bag it up, then?" Becky asked.

"Not if that means I have to take it off!" I said.

She and Mom laughed. "Today is not a good day to walk home in a ball gown," Becky said. "I have just the accessory for you." She reached into the glass cabinet up front and took out a tiny pair of peridot earrings. "They'll twinkle just a little bit in the mirror-ball lights."

I went to take the dress off, running my hand down it once more before handing it over to

Becky. Mom arranged to pick up the dress later that week when she had the car. After we paid, I slipped the earrings into my purse, a promise of the night to come.

"Have you talked with Rhys much since you agreed to go?" Mom asked on the walk home. "Are you going to have him match your colors? Maybe you should text him so he can get a tie or cummerbund that matches your dress."

"Good idea." I didn't mention that he was grounded from his phone for some unknown reason and that while Ian had my number, I didn't have his. "Or I'll tell him on Monday."

Chapter 40

The next week flew by pretty quickly. I had a lot of work to do—they always poured it on before the term break, which was coming after the May Day Ball this year in order to take advantage of the bank holiday. I had a lot of homework and was particularly proud of my essay on Katherine Parr, the last queen of Henry VIII and, as far as I could tell, the first Protestant Christian queen.

On Thursday I arrived at the paper office early so I could get everything delivered and still have time to study for a trig quiz. Natalie was there, typing away and ignoring the depressing vibe she radiated in every direction.

"Hi, Savannah," she said, starting a conversation with me for like the first time ever. I was immediately *en garde*, a new phrase I'd learned in French.

"Hi, Natalie." I went about my business, loading up my bag with that morning's papers.

"I hear you're going to the May Day Ball," she said. I looked up. "Melissa mentioned it."

I knew Melissa had been trying to be nice and show Natalie that I had plans for the ball even if they didn't include writing the article. Still. "I am."

"With Rhys Bowen."

Wow, she knew his last name. "Yeah. I didn't know you knew each other."

"We met last year," she said. "Before I moved. We'd consoled each other about how hard it was to move in secondary school."

Well, then. Rhys must have a thing for journalists. Or he'd needed help last year, too. Or he was a big player. Or he was nice to everyone. Or all of the above. He hadn't mentioned that he'd known her when he called her Nasty Natalie. Though come to think of it, I remembered his saying that he liked journalists. But that he didn't know any.

"That's nice," I said. Part of me thought, *You're two mushy peas in a pod*. The other part of me felt ashamed for thinking that about my friend and May Day date. Who had . . . lied to me?

I loaded the bag and prayed the entire time I made my deliveries. Not my usual prayers about keeping my Asking for Trouble column a secret or for Louanne or for this whole boy mess. I repented of the way I'd begun to think and speak and asked the Lord to help me, to give me the answer about what I should do to get back to being myself.

Chapter 41

Rhys found me after school. I didn't mention Natalie to him. For some reason I didn't want him to know that I knew.

"Hey, Savannah." He slid onto the bench alongside me. "I'm glad to finally find you alone. You're always surrounded with people, and we can never be alone."

"Busy week," I said. "I'm sure you've got a lot going on too."

"Yeah." He reached out to take my hand. I thought he was going to put something in it, so I let him take it, but then he enfolded my hand in his and squeezed it shut. I let my backpack slip off my shoulder so I could remove my hand from his to right it again. Then I slipped my hand into my pocket.

"Any chance we could hang out this week-end? to see a film or something?"

I shook my head. "Maybe . . . but . . ."

"As friends . . . good friends," he said. "Don't you ever go to movies with friends, Savannah?"

"It's my dad's birthday this weekend," I said. "I'm afraid I'm really busy. Sorry. We can talk Monday?" Two weeks till the dance. The money my parents had spent. The day-after garden and tea party. And I was a girl who kept her word. I was going to keep it to Rhys.

"Too bad," he said. "We could have had a good time. If you know how to have a good time, that is."

I looked at him.

"I'm just kidding." His voice was sincere, but his eyes were not. "Monday it is. I'll be thinking of you till then!" He grinned. I could still see the wolfish good looks that had originally drawn me to him, but I felt like maybe I was starting to see a glimpse of something more.

Or less.

Chapter 42

When I got home on Friday afternoon, Mom was already in a dither. "We have to hurry!" she squawked, then flapped around the rest of the house hanging black streamers and clots of black balloons. "He'll be home in an hour. Savvy—go check and see if the cake is done."

"Me? A cake?" I ruined everything in the kitchen. I even managed to wreck cereal, for crying out loud.

"Don't ask questions. Just do it!"

I did as I was told. I opened the smallish cooker—that would be oven, to us Americans—and looked at the cake. I jiggled the door handle a little, and the cake wobbled in the middle. That meant it wasn't done yet. Right? I jiggled the door handle a little more, and a small indentation fell in the center of the cake. I quickly closed the cooker door.

I'd told her not to have me check. "I don't think it's done!" I called out. Just then my phone vibrated. A new text.

Hey.

That was all it said.

I didn't recognize the number, and all my friends were programmed into my phone. Who was it?

Ian! I mean Rhys. Or Ian. I didn't know which, and I didn't have time to figure it out right then.

"Savvy! Please come in here and get rid of these shoes and this backpack and all the other junk you've left lying around." I heard the tone in my mom's voice. It meant *now*.

I ignored the text and gathered all my stuff into a large laundry basket and hauled it up the stairs. Louanne was lying on her bed. "Come on, we've got a lot to do."

"I know," she answered lethargically. "I'm hurrying."

"Hurrying like the dead?" This had gone on too long. I had half a mind to confront her right then and there, but my phone jingled. This time it was a ring and not a text. I checked the number. Ian again! I cut it off mid-ring. Louanne rolled off her bed and headed downstairs. I cleaned up my room and then headed down the stairs myself. Mom sat on the couch going over an invisible list.

"As soon as I get the cake out of the oven, we'll all change into our black clothes."

"Black clothes?" I asked.

Mom smiled for the first time that afternoon. "Yes. We're wearing black since it's Dad's fortieth birthday."

Well, now, that sounded fun. A clothing theme. I immediately started going over potential outfits in my mind.

"Then when Dad comes home, we'll yell, 'Surprise!' After he changes we'll head to Criminal Barbecue for dinner and come back here and open gifts and then—"

My phone rang again, loud. I couldn't take it anymore. I answered it and said, "Please do not call me anymore. I'm very busy!"

Mom and Louanne both stared at me. "Wow," Mom said. "That was kind of harsh. Who was that?"

"Rhys's stupid friend," I said. "Or Rhys. But I told him I was busy this weekend anyway."

"Oh," Mom said. I knew by her look that she thought I'd been rude. And, well, I had been. Which was not like me.

"Well, you girls go change. I'm going to call Aunt Maude and make sure everything is on for tomorrow," Mom finished.

"What?" I said. "Aunt Maude?"

"Yes, Savvy. Dad and I are going to Mercedes-Benz World in Surrey for his birthday and then for a late dinner out. Aunt Maude is coming to stay with you."

"Mom! I'm nearly sixteen years old. I can take care of us for the day."

Mom looked as though she were about to waver when Louanne spoke up. "Please let Aunt Maude come. I really want her to. Don't change anything." Her voice was pleading.

"Okay, we'll stick with the original plan," Mom said.

Louanne looked like the weight of the world had been lifted from her shoulders. She seemed to be ten years old again and not a hunched-over old lady like she had for the past few weeks. "Okay." She smiled. "Let's get changed."

Chapter 43

I'd never been to a fortieth birthday party before, but it was actually okay. I stuffed myself on barbecue and ate cake that had a slightly soggy middle—from hob jiggling, I suspect, but no one said anything. Dad loved his presents and wore his driving goggles all night to get ready for his test-drive at Mercedes-Benz World the next day.

I felt happy. And confident again, like I hadn't for quite a while. So I made a decision. Nothing more had come of the e-mail saying that someone knew my identity. It had just occurred to me that the person who wrote it probably didn't know me. It was sent to the Asking for Trouble e-mail address, after all. Who knows? Maybe it was someone trying to fake me out. I wouldn't answer the e-mail. If I did, *then* the person would be sure to know who I was.

Just the kind of bad journalism someone like Natalie was capable of. I wasn't falling for it.

Chapter 44

"Hullo, dears." Aunt Maude breezed into the house and hung her British nanny cape on the hook just inside the door. "I've brought the Stinking Bishop with me."

Louanne and I looked at each other. Then I discreetly went to the door as Aunt Maude headed for the kitchen. I opened the door and looked outside. No bishop there. Or pastor or priest or anyone else.

"Who did you say you brought?" Louanne asked sweetly.

"Not *who*, dear, *whom*. If you're going to speak English, please speak it properly. And in this case, it's not *whom*, but *what*." She reached into her bag and took out a large wedge of runny cheese wrapped in waxed paper. "Stinking Bishop. Smells bad but tastes lovely. For lunch, of course."

Louanne and I looked at each other and almost burst out in giggles.

"Come along, then. Let's have lunch, and then we'll make a plan for the rest of the day." She turned on the hob, then reached down and scratched Growl behind the ears. He immediately rolled over and bared his big belly for a tummy rub. She obliged, and Louanne burst into a smile.

Half an hour later we sat at the kitchen table. Aunt Maude served up the Stinking Bishop with a side of bread. Louanne, the vegetarian, dutifully ate some. If you asked me, it smelled like wet dog or Dad's gym socks after a long tennis match. I thought back to my science class. Lots of bacteria culture here. Lots. I dug into a flaky pie she'd set in front of me.

"Delicious!" I said, forking the crust and slurping up the gravy. "What is it?"

"Kidney pie, of course," Aunt Maude answered matter-of-factly.

Kidney pie. Of course. The kidneys had probably been taken from the organ donors buried in the back garden. Which reminded me . . .

"Aunt Maude, I have a favor to ask you. I won-der . . . I wonder if we might spend the afternoon cleaning up the back garden area."

Louanne dropped her knife and her jaw.

"Whatever for, dear?"

"Well," I answered, "Mom really likes to garden and, in fact, might be invited to join the Wexburg Ladies Association and Garden Club."

"My goodness, that's quite an accomplish-ment," Maude said approvingly. "I think it would be wonderful for her to spruce up the back with some new plants—breathe new life into the gar-den, as it were. And a lovely thought for you girls to do the work for her as a surprise for her return this evening. I'll sit outside and supervise. And whip up a little snack when you get peckish."

"No!" Louanne stood up so abruptly, her plate clattered to the floor.

Chapter 45

Aunt Maude and I looked at each other in surprise. Just as Aunt Maude was going to intervene, Louanne turned to me. "Savvy, would you please leave me alone with Aunt Maude for a minute?"

"Sure." I headed up to my room. What did they have to talk about that didn't include me? Could it be related, somehow, to Louanne's problem?

A few minutes later Louanne called me. "You can come down now."

When I walked downstairs, I was shocked to find Growl locked in his crate like a petty thief, staring at me—*me*, his archenemy!—to spring him, when two dog lovers had obviously locked him up.

Another surprise awaited me in the kitchen.

"Whose cat is that?" I asked with astonishment as I saw Aunt Maude holding a thin orange tabby.

Louanne sneezed. Twice. "It's bmine," she said, her nose already stuffing up.

"That's not your cat! You're allergic to cats. And so is Dad," I said, words slowing down as it all began to make sense. So this little guy was Louanne's big problem.

"How did this happen?" I said as the kitten cuddled in Aunt Maude's ample, soft arms and Growl actually did growl in the background.

"Well, one day I was taking the dog out in the morning, and this little thing was shivering by the back door. She was really skinny. I could see her ribs, just like they show you on the animal rescue shows on TV. So I went back into the house and got a little water and gave it to the cat."

"So then what?"

"Well, then I brought a towel for it to nest on way back where the garden is tangled, and it kept rubbing itself up against me to be friends, which made my allergies bad. And I got cat dander on my clothes. And then that got to Dad. And then he started having trouble too." She sneezed again, and Aunt Maude stepped back.

"Why didn't you tell us?" I asked.

"We don't know anyone here in Wexburg who could take a cat," Louanne said, shrugging her shoulders in a gesture that was more mature than her ten years. "I didn't want it to go to the pound. Where it might . . . *die!*"

Aah! So there was the inspiration for her Scrabble vocabulary.

"Bosh," Aunt Maude said. "We're not going to let this cat go to the rescue shelter. I'll just ring up a few people and we'll have her a home in no time."

Sure enough, while I washed and dried the dishes and Louanne blew her way through a whole box of Kleenex, Aunt Maude rung a few people. Half an hour later, Tabby had a home.

"I'll be back soon," Aunt Maude promised, swirling her cape around her as she breezed out the door.

While we finished the kitchen, I asked Louanne what finally made her ask for help. "The cat was starting to scratch me. And it was making me sick—and Dad, too. I wrote . . . well, I wrote in to the Asking for Trouble person at your school." She blushed. "I'm sorry, Savvy, but that's really why I was so interested in the paper. Not that I'm not interested in you, too."

"No problem," I said. "I had an extra reason for going to your dog show, too."

Her runny nose had slowed down now that Tabby was gone. "Anyway, that Asking for Trouble person told me to talk to someone who had the same values as me. Only I didn't know anyone else who loves animals like I do. Until Mom said Aunt Maude was coming. She does."

Yeah, Savvy. You'd better listen up too. Who do you know who shares your values? Who do you need to ask for help? Because it's not getting better; it's only making you worse.

Chapter 46

Monday morning at school, Penny pulled me aside. "Hey, Tommy just asked me for your number . . . again. Said he was pretty sure he'd written down the wrong one last time he asked me. I think Chloe overheard too."

"Did he say what he wanted?" I asked, remaining calm on the outside. On the inside, I was running over how my hair looked, if my lip gloss was fresh, and if my eyeliner could have smudged in this morning's typical mist.

She shook her head. "Nope, he didn't say anything more. I hope it's okay that I gave it to him." She looked slyly at me.

I punched her arm and went to class.

Chapter 47

Tommy didn't call Monday. Or Tuesday. I saw him in the hallway, and he waved and grinned. I knew I could ask Penny to find out from him what he'd wanted, but it seemed desperate and needy, and I didn't want to do it. If he had wanted to call me, he would have.

Wednesday night I was a little late getting into the coffeehouse, and I slipped in next to Supriya midway through worship. I hated missing worship. Joe caught my eye from the stage and nodded in my direction. I smiled. I knew he'd keep me in mind for worship someday. I just had to wait. My favorite discipline. Kidding!

I sang, and as I did, I imagined how it would be. One of the worship team members would become really sick—whoever that dude was up there who was playing guitar. No, no, that's not right. He would move! Or even better, he'd go on a long mission trip. Which would leave an opening for me. Joe would ask me to fill in with very little notice, and I would. I'd become a part of the team, and they'd invite me to join permanently, even when that other guy came back from, uh, Moldova or Lisbon or wherever he'd gone on a mission. And then Tommy would see me up on the stage and have great pangs of regret—

"Savvy!" Supriya tugged my arm. "Everyone else is sitting down."

I snapped out of it and looked around. I was the only one standing. I slid into my seat, making eye contact with no one on the way down.

Louanne had followed my advice. Shouldn't I follow my own? Who had my values?

Jenny. My newly assigned youth group leader.

I listened to Jenny chat about the lesson with us girls, and then when the groups broke up, I asked her if I could speak with her in private. "Of course, Savvy." We headed over to a couch in a corner of the room.

"So here's my problem," I began explaining to

her. "There's this guy I'm going to the May Day Ball with. But I'm really confused."

She didn't interrupt me but just waited patiently while I kept talking. I took a deep breath and went on.

"Anyway, when I first met him, I kind of felt sorry for him. He was new, he said, like I was. And I could help him, and he seemed very negative and I thought it would be good if I could share my faith with him."

Jenny nodded knowingly. I had the feeling she'd been there before, and it gave me courage to keep talking.

"So all my friends were going to the ball, and I didn't have a date yet, and my best friend wanted to invite my mom to something that she could only go to if I had a ball gown. So when this boy asked me . . . I said yes."

"I see," Jenny said. "But now you're sorry you did?"

"I am. Because the more I got to know him, the more sarcastic he got and he was cutting me down in little ways I couldn't exactly pin down. And he started wanting to be more than friends, even though I told him I didn't."

"Does he treat you with respect?" Jenny asked.

"Is he truly interested in you, or only in what you can do for him? Is he honest?"

I thought about that. He didn't really dis me, but whenever I was with him, I always ended up feeling worse about myself because of his little wounds. Kind of like . . . paper cuts. Which reminded me that he hadn't been really honest about Natalie either. "I don't think so," I said. "But I do know that I don't like how I feel most of the time when I've been with him. And I don't like who I've become lately."

Jenny opened her Bible to One Corinthians. "Remember when we studied this in our Corinthians series?" She pointed to a section. I read it on the page:

1 CORINTHIANS 15:33
Don't be fooled by those who say such things, for "bad company corrupts good character."

"Yeah, I remember that now," I said. I'd breezed right by it at the time, never thinking that anything like that could ever happen to me.

"Do you think that could be true in your case?" Jenny asked.

"Maybe. But what about all the money my parents already spent?"

"You could return your dress," Jenny suggested. "And the shoes and stuff, right?"

I nodded. "But they've already paid for the limo. And, well, didn't I give my word to him that I'd go?"

"You did," Jenny said. "But nobody agrees to be poorly treated. He also doesn't seem like he's taking you seriously when you said you wanted to remain friends."

I thought of his trying to hold my hand, his leaning even closer to, well . . . I wasn't sure. "You're right. I should probably have never gotten involved with him. So what should I do?"

"I can't answer that for you. But I can pray with you." We bowed our heads, and she prayed for me. I really didn't remember anything she said in the prayer because the whole time that one phrase from a teacher I'd had in middle school kept running through my head:

"The time to do the right thing is as soon as you become aware that it needs to be done."

203

Chapter 48

I was going to text him. I know, I know, cheap, low blow, cowardly. But I didn't actually do it. First, I had no idea if he had his phone back or not. I considered texting him on Ian's phone, but that seemed even worse. Instead, I thought I'd skip lunch on Thursday and meet him in the library.

Thursday morning I delivered the papers, as usual. I didn't take time to read my own and everyone else's columns; I would do that after school this time. I'd told Penny what I was going to do, and we made plans to hang out in the courtyard after school so I could fill her in on how it went.

I stepped into the library, half hoping Rhys wouldn't be there and I'd be off the hook.

He was there. I came up behind him at the computer. He sensed me and turned around and flashed that wide, white smile. "Hey, there's my girl," he said. "You've been so busy, I haven't seen you around much. I'm getting my phone back today, though!"

"Rhys, uh, could we go to the back of the library and talk for a minute?" My hands trembled, and I tried to take deep breaths without hyperventilating and passing out right there on the floor.

"Sure." He followed me to the back, to a nearly deserted section of the library among the musty biographies. As I looked at him out of the corner of my eye, I could still tell what I saw in him. He was cute, and he had a kind of . . . presence. People noticed when he walked by. But somehow the magnet that had once drawn me to him had completely turned around and was now repelling me a little instead. He plopped down on a bench and I put a few inches between us. He scooted over to erase the distance.

"There isn't an easy way to say this," I said, "but I can't go to the May Day Ball with you."

He faced me, shocked. "Your parents have told you that you can't?"

"No. I just realized . . . well, we're very different

people. And there are a lot of times I feel like you cut me down. You say things that are nice on one level, but there's always a little dig."

Rhys shook his head. "I thought you were big enough to take a little teasing, Savannah. I didn't think you were so oversensitive. I thought you were different."

His words confirmed to me that I was right to do what I was doing. I felt free. I felt affirmed. "I *am* different, Rhys—very different from the girl I've become over the past month or so. And I want the old me back."

"I've already paid for the limo," he said. "I can't give you your money back."

"That's fine. I'm really sorry about all this," I said, softening just a little when I saw the confusion on his face.

"Yeah, you *are* sorry," he said. I went to stand, but he put his hand over mine, keeping me on the bench for the moment. "You at least owe me a little token for our time together," he said. He leaned in close, and I could smell the rosemary mint of his shampoo and feel that charm he turned on to almost everyone around him. "How about a kiss good-bye?" His arm held me firmly— a little too firmly.

I wrested myself away from him and remembered what my mother had told me about firsts—first dances, first boyfriends, first kisses. I wasn't wasting any of those on Rhys. "I am kissing you off," I said. "But I'll never kiss you good-bye." With that, I took my messenger bag and began to make my way out of the library as fast as I could. The title of a Taylor Swift song ran through my head. *"Should've Said No."*

Before I was out of earshot, I heard him call after me, "She was right about you all along, you know."

I didn't turn around, but I did wonder. Who was *she?*

Chapter 49

I sat in the courtyard under the blooming wisteria, the age-old branches twirling around the posts and gripping them like an arthritic hand. Their perfume drifted down and enveloped me. I opened the paper and read a few of my friends' columns—Hazelle's in particular, which was actually very good. And then I read my own.

Dear Asking for Trouble,
It seems like for some reason a lot of things are going wrong in my life. My parents split up last year and we had to move to a smaller house (even though I'm still going to Wexburg Academy). Also, we were going to take a holiday to

visit my gran in Australia, and now we can't because of money. I don't want to sit around in the dumps all the time, though. Any advice?

Sincerely,
Blue

I clearly remembered reading this letter right after Tommy had mentioned my joy. Joy had been on my mind, and I'd based my answer on Psalm 126:5.

Dear Blue,
I'm sorry things seem tough right now—and none of these circumstances are your fault! Hold on, though. You know that saying "The dawn follows the darkest part of the night"? It's true. Try to find joy in the little things of life right now, day by day, and don't focus on the rough bits of choppy water that everyone needs to paddle through. Soon enough the sun will rise.

Sincerely,
Blue Skies

Someone slid in beside me. I looked up and blurted out before thinking, "You make a habit of sliding in next to girls, don't you?" First I was mortified I'd actually said it. Then I was happy that I felt free to say what I was thinking. The old Savvy was back!

Tommy grinned. "It would seem that way, wouldn't it?" He looked at the paper in my hands and folded it back to the AFT column. "I read that too," he said.

I kept my poker face on; I really did.

I could see Penny lurking, waiting for me, but like the great friend she was, she kept her distance. Tommy saw her too, though, and because he was a gentleman, he stood up to make room for her. He shook his shaggy brown hair, and I remembered again why I liked brunets. Then I remembered that he was dating Chloe and I locked the clasp of my heart.

"See you at the May Day Ball, I suppose?" he said.

I smiled, and he took that to be an affirmation. I wasn't going to spill my guts with him. And I hadn't even told Penny yet.

"See you Sunday." He waved at Penny and me as he took off.

Penny walked casually to my side and sat down. "What was that all about?" she asked. "Did he ever call you?"

I shook my head.

"Did he tell you what he was calling you about?" she asked.

I shook my head again. "He's just a nice guy, Pen. He probably had a question about our church or something and someone else answered it."

"Oh. Well, then. How did things go with Rhys?" She popped the lid off her water bottle, then took a piece of gum and offered one to me. I started telling her everything that had transpired.

"Creep," she said. "Well, you're still coming on May 2, right? to the garden and tea event?"

"I'd love to," I said. "But I won't have anything to wear. I can hardly expect my parents to keep my gown when I'm not even going to the ball."

Penny nodded. "Well, let me know what you decide to do. Whatever you want to do is okay with me."

"Thanks, Pen." I leaned over and hugged her. "I will. I'd better go home and talk to my mom about it now."

Chapter 50

Mom and I sat on the couch together, sipping tea—now iced tea instead of hot. "So that's the whole story," I told her.

She ran her hand through my hair, a soothing, comforting reminder of something she used to do when I was a little girl. "Are you happy with your decision?"

I thought about missing the whole night, about the fun that would happen. But then I thought about missing the garden and tea party. "I'm sorry we can't go to the garden party," I said.

"Me too," my mom said. "But totally understandable that you wouldn't want to go after all that."

"Oh, I don't mind going," I said. "It's just that I won't have anything to wear."

Mom set her glass of tea on the table next to the couch. "Why not?"

"Well, we'll have to take the Faerie dress back, right? I mean, it's too expensive to keep for nothing."

Mom shook her head. "It's not for nothing. You can wear it another time, to a wedding or something. The money spent isn't as important as the great decision you made and the amazing step toward womanhood you took. The dress is perfect for you. I don't mind keeping it if you want to."

"Really?"

"Really," Mom said. "And then I'll get a garden party out of it too. Speaking of which, I'd better get to the back garden, now that my wonderful girls have tidied it all up, and make a plan!" She stood up, and I went to call Penny and tell her that we'd be coming to the party after all. One good thing about not going to the dance was that I wouldn't have to stare at Tommy and Chloe dancing together all night.

When I picked up my phone, I saw that there was a voice message waiting for me.

"Savvy. It's Jack. Can you call me right away, please? Thanks very much."

Chapter 51

I dialed him before calling Penny. What could he want? "Hey, Jack, it's Savvy," I said. "What's up?"

"Savvy, thanks for calling me back so quickly. Listen, we've had a bit of a changeup, and I wonder if you can help the paper out of a pinch."

I almost said, "Sure, of course" automatically, but I'd learned to wait before saying yes. "What did you have in mind?"

"It seems that Natalie is not going to be able to take the photographs at the May Day Ball after all. She's, um . . . she's going to the ball now. I'd heard you were not going, and, well, I wondered if you'd reconsider taking the snaps that night."

Bad news certainly traveled fast. I had no idea how he'd heard that I wasn't going to be there.

I sighed. I was probably the only person on staff who wasn't going to the ball. And I did know how to take good photojournalism pieces.

He must have interpreted my long silence as a no, because he spoke up and sweetened the deal. "If you'll do this, I promise you'll have your own full-fledged article by the end of the school year. On whatever topic you choose. If we approve it, of course."

"With a byline?" I asked. If I was going to attend the dance in jeans and UGGs taking pictures of happy couples frolicking, it had better be worth my pain.

"With a byline," Jack agreed. "Will you do it?"

"Okay," I said.

"Thanks, Savvy; you're a lifesaver." And with that, Jack hung up.

I hoped I wouldn't regret this later. Only time would tell.

Chapter 52

Friday. Everyone was preoccupied with the ball. The campus was practically abuzz. Not wanting to get stung, I headed home right after school to bury myself in a good book. *Not* a romance.

Saturday. Helped Mom plant a few things in the back garden. Her joy lifted me up, and I actually started to look forward to the garden and tea party.

Sunday. Church. It rocked.

Monday. Louanne felt queasy, so I took Growl for a walk for her. He tugged at the lead the whole time and picked a fight with the neighbor's poodle. I must have been saving up a lot of do-good points for something. I hoped I'd actually get to cash them in.

Tuesday. Bumped into Natalie at the newspaper office. She said a noticeable nothing to me about taking the photos, and I said nothing either. Maybe Jack had taken her off the assignment?

The weekend was fast approaching. I was starting to feel a little queasy myself.

Chapter 53

Wednesday night I made it to church on time. I got a mocha. With extra whipped cream.

Jenny came up to me and asked, "So how are you doing?" I knew what she was really asking was *What have you decided about Rhys?* If it had been someone else, I might have thought they were being nosy, but not Jenny. She was my discipleship leader. She was supposed to ask me those tough questions.

I told her what I'd done, and she beamed. "I knew you had it in you, Sav. What about this Saturday? Going to watch a film?" she teased. I cringed, knowing that I'd given that same advice in the paper, and really, now that the recipient was me, it didn't sound as kind as it might have.

Live and learn, I told myself. This advice column business was on-the-job training.

"Actually, I'm going to the ball after all." I held my hand up to stop her before she could get too excited. "As a photographer. In the background. Wearing jeans and taking snaps of the happy couples."

"Oh, Savvy. Really?" Jenny said. "You okay with that?"

I nodded. "I am. Because the editor promised me an article next month."

We chatted for a few more minutes, and then Supriya and I stood next to each other for worship. Afterward Joe came onstage to announce the final winner for the April Fools contest.

It went to the lip-synchers. Of course.

Supriya leaned in and whispered, "I gave all my money to you."

I turned to face her and laughed. "And I gave all my money to you. We probably canceled each other out!"

During the devo, my mind wandered. I felt bad. Not only wasn't I able to give Be@titude the money for their event, but Natalie had e-mailed me that she'd taken out everything about them from the article.

Thinking about Natalie right then especially bugged me. I couldn't put my finger on why.

Chapter 54

I'd dressed for the part. Not the part I'd been expecting to dress for, of course. New jeans, white shirt, leather vest, gold hoop earrings. My hair was pulled into a long ponytail and gathered at the nape of my neck to keep it out of my eyes and out of the camera lens. Jack had given me the newspaper camera to use, and I'd been practicing with it all week so it'd be second nature to use it.

I sat on the couch, waiting for my ride. Mom came and sat next to me. "Are you up for this?" she asked.

"I guess," I said. "Not how I'd planned for this night to go."

"Lots of life doesn't go the way we plan it to,"

she said. "It's what you do when the plans change that matters."

I thought back to when Rhys claimed we were just friends but his actions made it clear that he wanted more. "I know," I said. "Expensive lesson."

"They almost all are," Mom said. "Ready to go?"

I nodded. We gathered up my stuff and left.

The ball was being held at Lallyworth Castle, a British National Trust property about twenty minutes away. There were several castles—castles, I tell you, not just mansions—within twenty minutes of my house. As far as I knew, the only castle on the West Coast of the United States was in California. I never stopped being amazed at being plunked down in a piece of ancient history.

Although The Beeches, Ashley's estate, was big, it was nothing compared with Lallyworth Castle. Someone had told me that Anne Boleyn and King Henry VIII had dined here. I closed my eyes and tried to imagine her feet walking up this very stone path.

The hospitality committee had set up a coat check in the entry hall, and they were already there, bustling about. I headed into the great hall, where the ball was to be held. The room was swagged in greenery and white roses, probably flown in from Spain. I'd take an extra picture of those for Mom. There were great crystal chandeliers hanging from the ceiling, already ablaze and warming the room. It was a good thing too, because several of the doors leading to porticos were open, letting in the evening air. It reminded me of a fairy tale. Only my coach had been turned into a pumpkin a week early.

The band was warming up, playing a mix of violin-tinged romantic classics and guitar-driven modern rock. I closed my eyes and imagined dancing. Then I went to a dark corner and set up the camera equipment so it would be unobtrusive and out of view for the ball's guests.

Couple by couple they came, and I snapped some photos, trying to have an emotionally detached reporter's eye and not thinking as a girl who had no date. About an hour in, Penny and Oliver arrived. She spotted me, left Oliver with some friends, and hurried over.

"You all right?" she asked.

"Fine!" I said brightly. Maybe too brightly. "Pen, you look beautiful. Divine. Oliver is the luckiest guy here." Her ears twinkled with the starry earrings she and her mom had found. Her silver-shot dress matched perfectly with the silver and crystal shoes. I didn't even want to know how much her mom had paid for those shoes. I didn't think her mom considered those things, really.

She beamed. "Thanks to your help in finding the dress—and Be@titude. Did you see . . . them?"

I didn't know which *them* she meant. "I assume they came with you." After all, Chloe was one of the Aristocats, and I knew that their whole group was having a pre-ball dinner together.

"With us? Why ever would they come with us?" She seemed genuinely puzzled.

"Chloe *is* one of your group, right?" I said.

"Ah . . . ," Penny said, grinning. "I had no idea that was who would be first on your mind. Though I should have. No, I mean—" she scanned the room and finally found whom she was looking for, then pointed—"them!"

Chapter 55

I followed to where she pointed and saw *them*. Rhys! With Natalie! At that exact moment, Rhys caught my eye, grinned, and then leaned in to kiss Natalie. She did not back away.

Even though I hadn't wanted to be here with him, I was shocked. I felt cold and my hands shook and I wanted to sit down. It all made sense now, and I should have figured it out much sooner. I felt betrayed. And then angry—my parents and I had paid to bring them here in a limo! And then . . . relief. I had dodged the bullet, as we Americans would say.

"Sav, are you okay?" Penny asked. "I've got to get back to Oliver."

"I'm fine," I said. "Have a great time. I'll take

some good snaps of you and see you tomorrow, right?"

"Right." She squeezed my arm, then glided back to her date and their table.

I hung out in the corner for a minute to steady my hands and then got back to work. I walked along the edges of the room and also on the outside porticoes, taking photos. I have to admit, I was scanning the room for another couple, even though I wasn't sure I wanted to see them.

But I did. Tommy looked fantastic in his tux and tails, as I knew he would. He had his hair trimmed just the tiniest amount so that it wasn't exactly short, but it was clear he'd attended to it for the night. Chloe's dress wasn't awkward, despite Penny's faithful protestations. She looked great. But she wasn't smiling. She was obviously angry. I suppose I should have been glad, because it seemed she was keeping a physical distance between her and Tommy.

Not wanting to be a stalker, I went back to work, heavyhearted, and stayed in the shadows. I promised myself I would not train my superzoom lens on them to see if they kissed or not.

The night went by more quickly than I'd thought it would, and people began to filter out of the ballroom. I was hanging in the back, resting. I'd taken enough snaps for the paper, for sure. I'd told the coat check people I'd stay and help them clean up afterward.

I heard a commotion and an angry, raised voice in one corner. I stood up to see where the noise was coming from. It was the corner where the Aristocats were hanging out. After popping off my lens cap, I aimed my camera in that direction. I wasn't snooping. I was a reporter. Right?

The group closed in around the commotion, keeping it as private as possible, and the voices had already been lowered. The band struck up another song to keep things moving along. If I hadn't had my superzoom, I probably wouldn't have been able to see what had happened. But I did have superzoom. Chloe had thrown her purse on the floor, where it still lay, and had turned her back to Tommy, who looked pleadingly at her at first; then he walked away.

I couldn't stand there like a CIA agent with my lens trained on them any longer, so I put the camera away. Shortly thereafter, their group dissolved, and about half an hour later, nearly everyone was ready to leave.

Lovers' spat, I thought with regret. I packed my

camera away and went to help the coat check guys break down the closet and tag the few coats that had been accidently left behind. They'd bring them to the school's lost and found the next week.

"Savvy, would you mind sweeping up the entry hall?" one of the guys asked.

"Not at all." I'd texted my mother, and she said she'd be here in half an hour.

I finished sweeping and then took my broom and stood in the ballroom, enjoying the music that the band generously kept playing while the hospitality crew cleaned up. I scanned the room, noting the painted frescoes on the ceiling, when I saw . . . Tommy! In the corner where he'd been sitting with Chloe and the others.

He caught my eye and, after reaching under one of the tables, came to where I was standing in the doorway. "Hey."

"Hey." I wished I hadn't been standing there gripping a broom. "I thought I saw you leave." *Oh!* I blushed furiously at that. Now he'd know that I'd been watching him!

He grinned. I'd been caught. But maybe it had helped him to be more honest himself. "I did leave—the boys took all the girls home. But I had to come back. My, uh, mobile phone had been lost. But I found it hidden in one of those." He swept a hand toward the thick puddles of velvet draperies spilling onto the floor.

"Lost?" I said.

"Well," he admitted, "Chloe had put it in her purse for the dance. And when she threw her purse, my phone went flying, along with everything else in her bag. I didn't want to hold up the whole limo looking for it. I forgot about it till the ride home."

I didn't ask, but he volunteered. "I'd told her when she asked me to the ball months ago that we'd just be going as friends, and she said okay. Bill and Maddie were going. Our whole group was going, and it seemed like it was going to be fun. But I guess, in the end, she wasn't really okay with it at all. The friends-only thing. She thought I'd change my mind about it between then and now, but I hadn't and, uh, it came to a head tonight."

I tried to keep the smile off my face. I was sorry for her—I was. But honestly? She'd acted like a brat several times now, and I didn't think she deserved him.

"Silly of me, eh, to think that would all work out?" Tommy asked.

"No," I said, "I understand perfectly." *More than you know.*

"So what happened to Rhys?"

I fished for the right words to say and finally hooked them. I looked at my broom and then up again, grinning. "Let's just say that Rhys is no Prince Charming. I came on assignment. Photo-journalism for the paper."

"So you didn't get to dance all night?"

"Afraid not. But it's okay. I came to do a good job, and I did. And," I said, particularly happy that I could share this news with him since he'd been telling me for months that he was looking for something I'd written in the paper, "Jack is giving me a full article next month. With a byline. I'll finally have something in the paper for you to read."

Tommy nodded. "Shame that you didn't get to dance, though." The band started a new song. "One of my favorites!" He took my hand and glanced at the other, holding the broom. "Put the mop and bucket away, Cinderella."

I dropped the broom and he led me just to the edge of the dance floor.

There were literally five people or fewer in the room, so I didn't feel self-conscious at all, and honestly, I probably wouldn't have noticed if there were hundreds of people. I didn't even remember what song was playing. In my mind, it was Taylor Swift playing "You Belong with Me."

I wasn't wearing my beautiful dress, and this wasn't how I'd planned it. But it was all the more wonderful for being unexpected. My first dance.

Afterward he smiled at me and I smiled back, and the band packed up. He headed toward the door; his dad was waiting for him in the parking lot. Just when he was still within earshot but too far away for me to respond, he turned back and said, "Oh, and, Savvy? I've already read quite a bit of your writing." With that, he laughed a little and waved good-bye.

I stopped dead in my tracks. *What?*

Chapter 56

We went to the first service the next day, but I didn't stay for Sunday school because we had to get home and get ready for the garden and tea party.

My phone buzzed twenty minutes before we were to leave. It was Penny.

> Be sure to do your hair in those long curls. And wear the earrings, too.

What was up with that? A small quiver of insecurity wavered through me, thinking that maybe she wasn't sure if we were good enough for her crowd. *I already talked to her about that,* I reminded myself. *I'm going to believe her.*

Shortly thereafter I stood in front of the mirror with the Faerie dress on. As I looked at it, I prayed for Becky and her ministry, and I knew—just knew—that my work with Be@titude wasn't over. It was only beginning.

I'd curled my hair in the long, loose curls Penny had insisted upon; the peridot earrings were buttoned in my lobes. When I went downstairs, my dad pretended to fall backward. "You can't leave the house like that! They'll take you to Hollywood. Or it'll cause a gun riot in the streets, with the boys fighting over you."

"They don't allow guns in England, Dad," Louanne drily reminded him.

"There aren't going to be any boys there," I said. "Only moms and girls."

He stood up and pretended to consider. "Okay, then," he said. "You can go." He came up and kissed my cheek, and I smelled his Old Spice and felt his scratchy whiskers. I hugged him back.

When we arrived at The Beeches, Mom asked, "Do I look okay?" She tugged on her dress a little and reapplied some lipstick.

"You look beautiful," I reassured her, realizing that I was in the strange position of having been here before, and with these people, while my mom had not.

We drove up the long, long drive of The Beeches and parked our Ford among the very swish cars that had already arrived. I thanked God that my dad had taken down the fuzzy dice from his rearview mirror and that Louanne hadn't let him put a bumper sticker on the back.

Once we were shown into the garden, though, all my fears melted away. First, Penny's mother came right over and took my mom by the arm and introduced her to everyone. Then she sat down with her at the table. It was clear that she'd saved a place just for her.

I beamed in appreciation as I went to the kitchen to meet up with the girls. Of course! What else would I expect from Penny's mum—like mother like daughter, right?

Several girls, including Ashley, commented on my dress, though none of them commented on the fact that I hadn't had a date the night before. Good manners.

The kitchen was abustle. We girls didn't prepare anything—the caterers had done all the food. We were just there to serve. Penny brought me a silver tray with tall glasses filled with sparkling pear cider. "Chloe's not coming today," she whispered. "Embarrassed by her tantrum last night, as well she should be." She sniffed. "Poor manners."

Once again I was reminded that my kind friend did have quite a lineage, and I loved her the more for being herself.

A violinist and a cellist played achingly beautiful music in the background, and we poured back and forth from the kitchen with full and then empty trays. After one trip, Penny asked me, "Could you please go to the entry hall and see if anyone has left glasses or dishes out there?"

I nodded, a little confused. As far as I knew, people had only been eating in the back garden area. And if they'd left things up front, wouldn't the butler have gotten them?

I walked into the hallway and there, in one of the corner armchairs, sat Tommy. He seemed stunned when I entered the room. I stopped, shocked myself.

"What are you doing here?" I asked.

"Waiting for my mum," he said. "She's the one on crutches," he explained. "Broke her foot last month. I need to help her up and down the steps. Penny asked me to get here a bit early—I thought maybe her foot was bothering her."

That Penny! As soon as she knew that Tommy was helping his mom, she'd texted me to do my hair.

"You look great," he said, still surprised, I thought, to find me in something other than jeans and boots.

"I clean up well," I teased, thrilled to have made an impression and ecstatic that he'd seen me in my dress after all. I knew I had just a minute or two before I'd have to go help, or someone was sure to come and find me. "Can I ask you something?"

"Sure," he said.

"What did you mean last night when you said you'd read my writing?"

He looked around to see if we were alone, and we seemed to be, except for the butler. "Your column. Every other week."

"How did you know?"

"I found some papers in the back of the church on April Fools night."

Oh! When my homework and papers were left out. How careless I'd been. "And you e-mailed me?"

He nodded. "But you didn't e-mail back."

"I didn't know if it was a trap." I could hear the

241

noise in the kitchen growing louder. It was time to get the puddings out, and I needed to hurry.

"And then I tried to call, but you answered and said not to call you anymore because you were very busy."

"That was you?" I was mortified.

"Uh-huh."

One of the girls came into the room. "Savvy?"

"Be right there," I assured her before turning back to Tommy. "I'm really sorry—I didn't know it was you."

"Not a problem." He grinned. "You'd better get back to the kitchen. Don't worry about it, though. I know how to keep quiet. Your secret is safe with me."

I knew it was. I waved a little and said I'd see him soon. *Really soon,* I hoped. And then I went back to serve dessert.

On the way home Mom chattered on and on about what a great time she'd had and how nice everyone was and how Mrs. Barrowman—Lydia— was going to sponsor her for the membership vote next month, and if she was in, they'd all do the Chelsea Flower Show together.

I let her have her moment, her half hour, of delight. I sat in the car and treasured up the day, and the evening before, to myself. When I got home, I'd search through last night's pictures and find the perfect one for my new screen saver. By an amazing coincidence I'd just happened to snap several dozen of Tommy without Chloe.

What an amazing weekend. First formal dress. First dance with a boy not related to me. What could lie ahead?

My promised article? An amazing ministry? My first kiss?

Hmm . . .

Your Father, who sees what is done in secret, will reward you.   MATTHEW 6:4, NIV

Straight from the streets of London and hot off the presses of the high school newspaper comes the new series London Confidential. Join fifteen-year-old Savvy and her family as they adjust to the British way of life after moving from the States. Experience the high-fashion world of London and learn about life in England—all while journeying with an all-American girl and budding journalist.

Along the way, you'll probably learn the same lessons Savvy does: it's better to just be yourself, secrets can be complicated, and popularity comes with a high price tag!

Giving advice to others is one thing.
It's another thing to find out that God expects
you to live out those lessons yourself. . . .

Read the entire series!

Book #1: *Asking for Trouble*
Book #2: *Through Thick & Thin*
Book #3: *Don't Kiss Him Good-Bye*
Book #4: *Flirting with Disaster*

For more information on London Confidential,
visit www.tyndale.com/kids.

CP0974

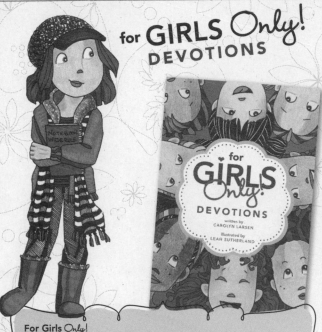

for GIRLS Only!
DEVOTIONS

written by
CAROLYN LARSEN

illustrated by
LEAH SUTHERLAND

For Girls Only!
This devotional gets right to the heart of many topics you face:

- feeling like you don't measure up
- dealing with gossip
- trying to face your fears

Through Bible verses, stories about real issues, and self-quizzes, this devotional is a fun way to learn more about living out your faith in real life.

Filled with cool sketches and easy-to-understand devotions, *For Girls Only!* is a great tool for spending time with God and finding out more about yourself!

For more information, visit www.tyndale.com/kids.

CP0386

LOOK FOR THESE
ONE YEAR® PRODUCTS
FOR YOUR FAMILY!

 The One Year®
Devotions
for Kids

 The One Year®
Devotions
for Kids #2

 The One Year®
Devos for Girls

 The One Year®
Devos for Girls #2

 The One Year®
Devotions
for Boys

 The One Year®
Devotions
for Boys #2

 The One Year®
Did You Know
Devotions

 The One Year®
Did You Know
Devotions 2

www.tyndale.com/kids

CIP0914